I0589786

BULLIES INC.

the book your parents don't want you to read

STEVE DIMARCO

SMART HOUSE BOOKS

Smart House Books
Toronto, On.
www.smarthousebooks.com

Publisher's Note: This is a work of fiction. Names, characters, places, and incidents are a product of the author's imagination. Locales and public names are sometimes used for atmospheric purposes. Any resemblance to actual people, living or dead, or to businesses, companies, events, institutions, or locales is completely coincidental.

Editor, Heidi von Palleske, Smart House Books
Book Layout © 2017 Smart House Books
Cover Layout, Aaron Rachel Brown

ISBN 978-0-9689718-4-0

To any who I might have bullied
I am truly sorry
To any who might have bullied me
I'm sorry for altogether different reasons

36 across: five letter word for terrorist?

B-U-L-L-Y

All those motherfuckers better hope I'm never diagnosed with a terminal disease.

I was surrounded by it, choking on it, their brutality, their belittling and violence against those weaker. Their fucking PDA's, *Public Displays of Affliction*. Bullying is terrorism, pure and simple. My high school thinks the appropriate punishment for a bully is to suspend them for two days. Yeah, and let's give the serial killer a weekend pass from death row. Party on dudes!

I could no longer stand by and watch the atrocities go unpunished. I had to do something. But exactly what?

'Now, sit back, relax, and think of nothing...'

Really? Think of nothing? My psychiatrist demanded that not ten minutes into my first session. I did not go to him voluntarily. After everything went down dad sent me to him in an effort to mold, or skin me, into a more social being. Someone more like everyone else.

Like when I worked in the fish and chip shop wearing the cheesy uniform as everyone else. My job was readying the potatoes for the fryer and we had this skinner, a round tub that's insides were coarse stone, where one threw in the spuds, turned it on, and off with their skin. Thing is all these different looking potatoes (I came to learn potatoes are as unique as snowflakes) came out skinned and molded into looking exactly alike. As if they'd spent time with a shrink.

'Dolf.'

As my crimes are still under the statute of limitations, I need to use a pseudonym. *Dolph.* It's short. Has no ring to it. Definitely not the heroic ring of many a pseudonym. In no way do I consider myself a hero: regular, anti, super, or any other variety. I don't believe in fucking heroes! There was no revenge, no retaliation in what I did. I had never been a victim of bullying.

I'm going to share my Bullies Incorporated journey, journeys really, but I'm going to recount it as one, same as a hundred battles compromise one war. And if it ever gets too difficult, just sit back, and think of nothing...

2

For different legal reasons, I will tag my byline under an alias. I'll stick to initials. I could almost use my own, they are commonplace letters, one vowel, one consonant. But better to be safe. N.W.

I was still new to journalism, something I'd wanted from a very young age. 'Too young' said my mother who saw me on a war front, prisoner of some, and I quote: Degenerate war faction who'll gang-rape you for months on end, and when they're through with you they'll saw off your head and place it on a pike! Unquote. My mother has always had a flair for the dramatic. One never raised one's voice, 'They wailed like lunatics!' One was never tight for cash, 'They were reduced to paupers!' One never apologized, 'They groveled on their hands and knees for my forgiveness!' I will not write in that key.

At the time of Bullies Inc., I was reporting on local events, life's more upbeat items; first newborn of the year, golden wedding anniversaries, people celebrating centenarian birthdays. I was searching for that breakout story, something that would propel me from the newborn/geriatric hit parade of local banalities. Something I could sink my teeth into.

Bullying has been on the news radar for a very long time. The stories pretty much carbon copies of one another, some bullying verbal, some physical, some via the Internet, all with the same tragic overtones. Like most children, I was bullied. And for the record, I was once a bully. I became one of a throng of bitter girls casting their bitterness onto others. But before that, before gaining acceptance into their clique, it was those very same girls who had bullied me. The hunted becomes the hunter. Not a yearbook moment.

In any case, during my reporting of the city's banalities, I stumbled upon a story that sounded like the concocted plot of some straight-to-DVD movie. I realized that if it were only half true, it could be my ticket out of banality land to becoming a back bencher; journalist speak for Sr. reporter, and maybe another step towards having my head mounted on a pike.

3

A mother ingesting her problematic litter, is there anything so pure?

Vultures casting shadows over what they wait to die. Is there anything so candid?

Does a cockroach do anything other than hurl its entire existence into staying alive?

I found myself incapable of leading any other life than that of an animal. Now I don't mean in that yuppie posturing way, the au-neo-natural parents keeping their child's afterbirth in the freezer. What happened to just bronzing baby shoes? Or peeling open their baby's soiled diapers and reading them like they would a Rorschach blotter. I too doubted that kind of thing – Go TV! No, I went for animalism in its truest form. Instinct, nothing but pure, unapologetic instinct.

I'd watched bullying grow both in occurrence and prominence. For that I blame the fucking media who in their efforts to gain our attention and therefore advertiser $, insist on making headlines out of them, thereby turning them into deviant, underground pop stars.

'Fuck dude, did ya see I was on the news last night? Well I wasn't totally on the TV, but the kid I smashed up was! He better not rat me out... But like they were talkin' 'bout me on fuckin' TV dude!'

Instinct decreed something must be done about this. And I don't mean ratting, tattling or in any way informing on them; not that I have anything against that type of thing, I mean if one is overwhelmed and has no other choice than ask for help, of course they should. But all I've ever seen following those cries for help are the bullies getting the aforementioned suspensions, or other wrist-slaps.

My goal was to level the playing field, to produce a series of interventions that would strike fear into all of them. An eye for an eye typa thing. And who out there doesn't want to see a bully go down, and go down hard. Perhaps go down and never get up. Okay scratch that last one.

But can you really scratch that last one? You know the way lawyers say something they shouldn't, and the other lawyer objects, and then the judge tells the jurors to disregard the last statement. Right, just disregard it. And when you master that, you can sit back and think of absolutely nothing...

4

For now I think it best I get out of the way. I'll be back when it's relevant.

5

A heart can be broken a thousand times, a spirit only once.

My first recruit would be the toughest, and the most vital. I mean in gaining their trust, in making them believe in my concept, and therefore believe in the success and rightness of Bullies Inc. If I failed at this, the entire thing would collapse.

I will pseudonym this first recruit – Van Detta.

When he was younger Van Detta had been a primary victim of bullying. But a growth spurt in his twelfth year suddenly cast shadows over his bullies, and they turned their freshly battered faces to less threatening marks. Van's new, primate-like physique (not quite the missing-link but evolution seemed to have skipped a beat) became something to be feared.

Bullies Inc.'s first target would be a neighborhood boy/asshole. Again I refuse to mention any names or specifics at the risk of tipping off the authorities.

Fucking authorities with their decaled car doors: *To Protect and Serve*. But without the support of clandestine rat-lines, canine slave-labor, and criminals trading down their crimes: 'For immunity on the robbery – I'll give you two drug dealers. Three beatings – I'll raise ya a dismembering!' Yeah. *To Deflect and Swerve*.

Anywho, I plied Van Detta with inspirational speeches on the rightness and virtuousness of what we could do, all we would accomplish. Sadly my communications, no matter how impassioned, washed over him like tax dollars through government fingers.

So I did what any corporation would. I paid him. And in that transaction Bullies Inc. officially came into being.

6

Round one...

Finances settled; Van Detta and I began preparation on Bullies Inc.'s first offensive. I'll call him Ralph. Ralph was your average bully, no twists or kinks to his work, no sparkling witticisms or tortures, nothing that would get him on first ballot into the Bully Hall of Fame. Ralph was a meat and potato bully.

I'd briefed Van Detta with Intel gained from school gossip and facts I'd secretly gathered on Ralph. These facts I kept in a notebook, my Bully-dossier, secreted away in the hollow of my great-granddad's wooden leg. This yellowed family heirloom, kept in GGD's honor, stood peg-like in the dark of my father's bedroom closet. During the First World War GGD had his leg blown off. His war records referred to it as having 'lost it.' Who loses a fucking leg? 'Think man, where was the last place you saw it? It has to be around here somewhere. It couldn't have just gotten up and walked away.'

That's the kind of thing my dad would say. He's a lawyer. Yeaaaaah, a lawyer. And yes he believes he's doing the world a world of good. But his grade of legal shark can be one of life's nastiest. Acing his job means one of the divorcees being fucked out of wealth, humility, and occasionally spirit. But lawyers are trained to hide all empathy behind the eternally unbalanced scales of justice. Who else but adults would blindfold their overseer of justice?

He runs our household much like he runs his business, only at home he's less lawyer and more judge.

'Dad, can you pass the potatoes?'

'Overruled. Finish your vegetables.'

'I hate broccoli.'

'Overruled! Broccoli is one of earth's super foods.'

Staring down into her plate, my mother would weigh in, 'Please just eat your broccoli dear. It'll save us all – '

'Sustained! You heard your mother. Eat your broccoli!'

I also have two siblings. Less about them later.

I could not risk Van Detta being recognized, so I asked my mother to put together – under the guise of giving it to a friend's father for his birthday – a bowling ball bag. Feeling needed, my mother's sewing needle took to the air.

Yes, I could have just bought a sack and cut out two eyeholes. But having my mother make it? Involving any of my pacifistic family members in my bully cleansing? The thought still leaves me tingling.

Despite having cut out a mouth and two substantial eyeholes, it turned out Van Detta had acute claustrophobia and after only a few seconds in the hood he'd pissed himself and torn it to pieces. Walking away, he swore he'd come up with his own disguise. 'My own disguise to disguise me!'

We still hadn't worked out the specifics of our offensive. Was it to be a series of backhanders? A pummeling of fists? A laying of boots? As Ralph's bullying used no weapons, I allowed no weapons. Besides, he could make a case of any weaponry against him, and draw undo sympathy.

I'd written a Bullies Inc. proclamation, the gist, If Ralph did not cease and desist his bullying, incidents like this would both continue and worsen. I'd hoped Van Detta might verbally pass on this message (as Ralph lay broken and helpless in the alley) but Van Detta and proclamations (words in general) really didn't mix. A letter it would be.

I won't bore you with all the planning that led up to Bullies Inc.'s first offensive, to Ralph's life lesson, but as he raced his ten-speed down his usual alley, kicking the side mirrors off any and all parked cars, Van Detta speared a hockey stick into his front spokes. The bike flipped over in a complete circle, leaving Ralph spread-eagled on the asphalt, groaning in pain and crying for help. From my perch on a fire escape I watched Van Detta approach. Ralph tried to get up, but collapsed back to the ground.

Van Detta stood over him, silent and still as a statue. I watched. I waited. Ralph cried out for help, for the paramedics. Van Detta remained. I began to shake, maybe even more than Ralph. I wanted to call down to Van, 'Deliver the fucking letter!' but I was too scared.

Then I heard Van clear his throat. He asked Ralph, whose cries were mounting, which foot he used to kick the kids he bullied. That was Ralph's preferred method and why he always wore steel-toed boots. Ralph claimed he didn't know what Van Detta was talking about. Van Detta said something of hating being dissed, and raised a fist. Ralph wailed for mercy. I never knew a sound so pathetic could be so uplifting. As my granddad used to say: 'It'd bring a tear to a glass eye!' Ralph begged Van Detta to call an ambulance.

But my proclamation! Ralph needed to know why this happened and if he continued bullying it would happen again. Having landed on his stomach, Ralph was finally able to turn himself over onto his back. His scream was gut wrenching. Oh, Van Detta did go with a disguise, the only thing open enough not to invoke his claustrophobia, a baseball umpire's mask.

I can guess what you might be thinking, why didn't I ever step up when Ralph was putting the boots to someone? Simple, I was too afraid. But in hindsight I'm glad, for if I blew off some steam then... Well that steam of outrage is what drove me to form Bullies Inc. Better an organized multitude of assaults than one lone bravery.

Van Detta did not raise his voice nor once try to compete with Ralph's mounting cries, he just kept repeating, almost robotically, 'What-foot-do-you-use?' When Ralph finally admitted which foot, Van Detta's next action almost caused me to topple off the fire escape.

Van Detta stretched out Ralph's right leg then leaping into the cool night air came down on his foot. I not only heard the crack of bone, I felt it. By this point I was so panicked I'd forgotten about the letter. I just wanted out of there. But Van Detta, who continued to impress me with his steely focus, hadn't forgotten and stuffed the envelope into Ralph's yowling mouth.

12

At home in bed the scene played over and over in my mind, cut into little pieces like a movie trailer. And like any good movie trailer, it left me wanting more...

7

ONE DOWN...

My school was one of the first to fall under the banner of zero-tolerance. Once a bully was reported, after listening to the victim, and then the indignations of the 'Falsely' accused bully, the principal would ask for some kind of corroboration, a witness or two to the alleged crime. If no one presented themselves (most refused to get involved) both parties were dismissed, but not until the victim was made to shake hands with the bully. So the bully is not only set free, he's now stoked with hand-shaking vengeance.

On one occasion the principal insisted the victim and bully not only shake hands but hug out their 'misunderstanding.' This was as wrong a move as could have happened. The bully was hugely homophobic and had been bullying the kid for that very reason, for the kid being 'Queer.' I won't go into what the kid suffered at the hands of that, but neither he nor any other gay student ever again broached the principal's office. That became the real zero tolerance.

If a cop is shot at, does he scurry behind his logoed cruiser door, *To Infect and Deject*, and begin a dialog with the perp on the evils of cop killing? 'Hey there, big guy, just you hold up a second. Now I wanna say there's only one thing getting in the way of you and me becoming good friends. Yeah, it's that thing in your hands. That's right, you know what I'm talkin' about. That assault rifle with the extended clip.'

They fucking fire back! When most countries are attacked do they spend hours upon hours at the UN (the adult version of the principal's office) trying to hug it out? NO. They retaliate. You started it, we'll fucking-well end it! I was doing nothing more than taking a page from the book of ADULTS. Subscribing, not to 'Do as I say, not as I do,' but: 'Do as I do!'

Safe to say Ralph's victims were no longer victims. In fact once Ralph was far enough along in his physiotherapy, once he hobbled back to school on his aluminum crutches, inching along the corridors, his every totter announced by the squeak of rubber crutch feet, he would not even raise an eye to his former prey. Turned out old Ralphy could actually read (I had my doubts) because the last part of the warning letter proclaimed any eye contact with his former victims would incite further realigning. From this point on I'll refer to these encounters not as interventions, but realignments.

Though I never would have thought to do it myself, I found a kind of simple genius in Van Detta's point of focusing on Ralph's foot, punishing the body part he used in his bullying. It was fitting, logical, and perhaps even a little poetic. Adding to his demise Ralph was shunned by his former groupies. Yeah, poor discarded, lonely Ralph – '*Bring a tear to a glass eye.*'

8

I announce my retirement...

Bullies Inc. I'd borrowed the name from an old subsidiary of the Mafia called Murder Inc., also an unregistered and unnumbered corporation. Not the most creative of names. If I'd started one against homosexuals, for whom I hold no ill feelings, I could have christened it with a little more flair like, Seize the Gay. Or, against the aged, Seize the Grey. But at the time Bullies Inc. was the best I could do, and what's in a name anyhow?

As great as Bullies' first offensive was, my fear of being caught blossomed into outright paranoia. I mean, with dad being a lawyer and, me being a criminal, where would that leave him? 'Father of Bullies Inc. founder disbarred!'

I love my dad. Sure there's some things I don't like, his court-like stiffness, his occasional inappropriateness and corny jokes, but those things aside he's a good guy. Great provider, caring husband and father; the type of things that are either taken for granted (save for the Hallmark-enforced Father's Day) or simply not there. And yeah, dad thinks he's a comedian, a vocation he would've pursued were it not for his own father, a lawyer.

I'll share some of dad's comedic stylings. Once in a restaurant, this was no McDonalds, strictly dress code and glitz, he caught a glimpse of the chef, a very attractive woman and promptly announced, *'I'd like to caramelize her onion!'* He actually said that.

At first shocked by the quip, my mother surrendered a laugh, one she likely still regrets, for it kicked open the long-sealed door of my father's comedic yearnings. After that our family couldn't enter a restaurant without the accompaniment of one of my father's culinary zingers, first aimed at the chefs, but with them rarely in eyeshot, he lowered his boom to waitresses and busgirls.

'I'd like to ball her melon!'

'I'd like to grate her cheese!'

'I'd like to sauté her veal!'

'I'd like to steam her clam!'

There were more, but I think you get the point. And if you don't you can 'Marinate my leavings!'

Anywho, one night at the dinner table, surrounded by my siblings and parents, I silently vowed to withdraw Bullies Inc. from any future realignments. That weight off my shoulders, I looked upon my family with newfound love...not so much love but reserved fondness, especially for dad. I even felt a quiver of affection for his cornballs of wit. But somewhere in my penchants I missed the dinner table's change of conversation.

The subject of my first realignment was being discussed. Ralph's injuries had attracted much attention; his parents, the police and some of the medical profession disbelieved his ankle could have been so badly crushed in a fall off his bike. People were seeing Ralph as the hapless victim of bullying. I wanted to leap up and say *HE WAS THE FUCKING BULLY* and got what he deserved! But before I could, dad broke down weeping.

All eating, all conversation stopped. Watching my father, I felt I was watching a total stranger. I'd never seen him cry before and his tears both moved and scared me.

Turned out as a child he'd been a victim of bullying. Yeah, a real fucking target, the kind where people who would never think of bullying happily joined others in his torture. Face in hands he cried for that big brother who never came to his defense (not that dad ever had a big brother). His tears drew tears from my sister then tears from mom who, up from their chairs, flanked my father in commiseration while my little brother swore vengeance against the culprits!

I'd never been so close to a victim's miserable anxiety, or witness to their broken, pathetic cries for help. I was overcome. There was my little brother ready to take on any and all comers. And me? I was nothing but a frightened corp. head, covering my ass against what hadn't even happened! What kind of coward was I?

Right then, in the flood of dad's wretched tears, I decided rather than continue my withdrawal, I would amp up Bullies Inc. and throw my very existence into it. My next realignment would be dedicated to dear old Dad!

9

Intervention Divine...

With Bullies Inc.'s retirement being about as long as most rock band's retirements, I didn't have time to quell my fears, that of being caught and dragging dad down with me, or the more immediate one of Van Detta. How did I know he wouldn't turn me in, or just plain old turn on me? The way a disgruntled postal employee comes after his workplace with an assault rifle or grenades, though that attribute seems to have extended into many other areas of employment.

Before I could really get it up to go back into battle, I got a text from Van Detta to meet him that night in the park. Had he picked up on my worry? Was he about to turn his unbridled aggression against me and stomp me down to rubber-footed crutches?

I travelled to the woods in terror, barely able to breathe, my short life flashing before me (not a moment remotely intriguing). What was it about? What did he want? Was Van Detta about to blame me for getting him into all this? I dialed 911 and, phone in hand, was one press away from help. A crashing through the woods had my heart in my mouth, and my finger yearning into *Send.*

More crashing. I could imagine only Bigfoot sounding as loud, though not as aggressive. Plowing through the last stand of greeneries, Van Detta. The expression on his face was stranger to me, neither cold nor vacant nor angry, rather it seemed distorted with thought. What he did next, what he spoke of, was nothing I could have guessed or even dreamed.

Seemed Van Detta lived near Ralph who, following his afterschool physio, took to sitting on his front lawn, reading a leather-bound copy of the Bible. Ralph's parents were devoted churchers and, with him limping remorse, were finally able to reel him back into their fold. Hallelujah!

Van Detta wandered past enough times that old Ralphy (unable to recognize Van without the umpire's mask) called him over and the two were soon reading from the good book. (The Bible, life's lint-brush for guilt and regret.) Van Detta then declared sin was the 'Devil's chain of arrangements.' Is there anything that Bible doesn't know?

Wiping cold beads of sweat from my temples I looked into Van Detta's eyes trying to read where he was going with this. He admitted to being frightened of being caught, not by the authorities but the higher power, and was equally afraid of becoming addicted to the power of realigning of bullies. A hallowed look clouded his face and Van Detta told me he and Ralph were in the midst of organizing funds for a summer bible camp.

Like the second your finger jabs through toilet paper, I was seized by astonishment and grimaced. Sure we've all heard the stories; the prisoner or hooker or drug addict falling on their knees and begging the higher power for a second chance (have you ever heard of someone winning the lottery and suddenly embracing the higher power) but Ralph and Van Detta teaming up in the name of the Lord?

Van Detta looked straight into me and said, 'Matthew 5:38, an eye for an eye and a tooth for a tooth.' Before stomping off he said: 'I will carry on our work, not for money, not for vengeance, but for the goodness of Man. Donations to the bible camp will gladly be accepted.'

I preferred a better place for the money to go, but.... Inspired, I set sights on a new candidate, and it turned out, a superior of Ralph's. This asshole's personal wave of terror reined not only over the weak, but other bullies. Cut the head off the alpha-bully and the rest might follow?

10

Glass Through the Looking...

I live in a small city. I don't mean a village (though it's certainly thriving with idiots) but definitely no NYC. My next realignment, I'll tag him with the pseudonym Joe-Bow, was someone marginally connected to my family; some years back my dad had been his father's divorce attorney. Seemed Joe-Bow's father was surreptitiously inhabiting a 'men's club' and one night after a particularly long run of Whiskey-sours and table dances, invited two of the 'dancers' to a private room, where they were to continue plying their trade to him and him alone.

Joe's drunken father woke up to the strippers in their kimonos, flanked by two massive bouncers who promptly informed him of the evening's conclusion, but before he could go anywhere there was the matter of his bill, two girls for two hours and fifty-three minutes, which totaled twenty-three hundred $, unless he was considering adding a tip. With his credit card maxed, and no friends he felt quite right about calling at 4 in the morning, Joe's father had little choice but to call his wife.

Now I know all that tragic shit about children of divorce, but does that give young Joe-Bow (he is in fact Joe Jr.) or any other divorce casualty reason to terrorize and humiliate others, others inevitably of smaller stature and gentler demeanor?

His modus operandi came in three stages. Joe began his terrorization by staring at his victims, staring as if he might hold some strange fondness for them. Having put them off guard he'd start yelling at them, screaming millimeters from their face, terrifying them with threats of physical violence and online humiliations that would inevitably conclude with his victims surrendering pretty much anything Joe-Bow demanded. He'd relieve them of whatever $ they had on hand, their phones or tablets (which he sold on his own black market) and make it a day-to-day ritual until the victim was broke, both financially and emotionally.

Often the first two steps took care of business. But when staring and screaming weren't enough, when a teen decided to stand up to him, bravely refusing him any money or electronics or fear, Joe-Bow knocked him unconscious with an elbow to the jaw (hence the Bow of Joe-Bow).

Clearly we're not talking any fly-by-night bully. Joe-Bow was the epitome of Bullies, the kind if there was ever to be a statue or mountain sculpting, like mount Rushmore, Joe-Bow would be there, chin held high, scowl etched across his face.

I knew if Bullies Inc. were to thrive and survive I could not have its realignments as open and reckless as our first, leaving someone screaming in an open alley. Bullies Inc. needed to function with much more discipline and control. Pondering this I was reminded of my most treasured subway ride.

As the train pitched and screeched through the tunnel, I watched two teens act out all the stereotypes that give teenagers a bad name: openly swearing, trying to outdo each other in gross name calling, knocking each other into other passengers then blaming the other for the mishap. These boys were true human accomplishments.

Taking a break from their endeavors they rode between subway cars smoking cigarettes. Soon that defiance was not enough and they began spitting at each other. Like rain these droplets grew in size and with some heavy hawking became thicker and fuller. Their conflict was brought to a sudden breath-halting end when one of the gluey missiles grafted-to the dress pants of a businessman. The teens froze. I froze. We waited for the businessman to look up from his newspaper, but oblivious to the situation he continued analysis of the financial section. The ride carried on with nothing more of note, until we reached the main transfer station. By then the teens, no doubt exhausted from their endeavors, sat by the doors playing on their phones. The businessman rose, folded the newspaper and took his place by the doors. When the train stopped people pressed by him, jostled him, but he stood fast in the doorway.

A whistle warned the doors were about to close. Mr. Businessman drew an arm back, formed a quick fist, and drilled the teen that hit him with the hork straight in the face. The kid's head careened off the wall behind him and he hunched down, blood decanting from both nostrils. I looked back in time to see the businessman stepping onto the platform, the doors closing behind him. And as the train pulled out from the station I craned my neck for as long as I could, until he was long from sight. I'd never witnessed such control. I didn't think it even possible.

This plain, unadorned businessman would be my muse, my inspiration. Bullies Inc. needed to learn his kind of control. Sadly, Van Detta was unmoved by my recounting of the incident. 'I never take the frickin' subway.'

Though indifferent to the tale, I made it clear we must operate in a similar fashion to the Businessman: so plain as to be invisible, so self-assured as to be invincible. Having already formed a rash plan to deal with Joe-Bow, I decided to put him on the back burner (if I only had a burner on which to put him) until I felt his realignment was at par with my muse. It would not take long.

11

Hey Joe where ya' going with that fate in your hands...

Joe-Bow's bullying not only continued; it amplified. Forgoing his foreplay of staring and screaming, Joe was down to just throwing elbows. Meanwhile Van Detta was chomping on the bit, needing to right the world's evils, eye-by-eye, tooth-by-tooth, by.

As fate would have it Joe-Bow, who pedaled his hijacked goods throughout the neighborhood (the earlier mentioned smart phones and tablets) offered me one of his unsavory bargains. Well it wasn't really fate; in school I'd put word out I was looking for a tablet and was face to face with Joe in less than an hour. Looking up into his icy-brown eyes I became fearful not only of him, but that buying into his perversion would - if my realigning failed - incite him into worse bullying.

He gave me that famous Joe-Bow stare, eying me up and down as if a friend, then gauging me with a look of: *I know the secret you don't want anyone else to know.* Normally this would have penetrated me, froze me, made me only want to please him. But not then, for flanking me (at least in spirit) was 'Nails,' my pseudonym for the subway Businessman. I made the appropriate nervous gestures and twitches and having the desired effect, Joe-Bow took me into his confidence, allowing me to give him a 30-dollar deposit on a 120-dollar tablet.

The transaction was to occur in the woods near our school. Waiting for Joe-Bow to arrive I scoped out the area for realignment suitability. It was bounded by bush and trees which kept us concealed from the surrounding streets, but what if someone where hidden amongst the shrubbery, some homeless person or cruising pedophile? What then?

Joe-Bow was late. Not fashionably, but arrogantly. He produced the tablet and I the balance of the purchase. As Joe counted and recounted the 90$, he had me turn it on. The screen saver was a photo of the tablet's previous owner sprawled on the ground with a bloody mouth; prominent in the foreground an elbow, one I could only assume was Joe-Bow's. 'Nice.' I actually fucking said that, 'Nice.' Joe agreed and said if I were to ever think of ratting him out, I'd get even worse. Missing teeth and dentistry were also mentioned. I nodded thinking the only dentistry that would occur, save for my bi-annual cleaning, would be in his fucking, unsparing yap.

I let some days pass then contacted Bow. I offered to fence whatever electronics he could accrue and pay top dollar. I gave him a deposit of 150$.

I set up our transaction for the next week. Joe-Bow wanted it sooner, as did I, but on the brink of agreeing with him I thought of Nails, and how he'd probably, if he knew of Joe-Bow's impatience, make him wait. Let him get settled by the subway door unawares, so to speak.

As fate would have it, the night called for thunderstorms. I love thunderstorms. Van Detta, not so much. At age 12 his mother sent him to the local pub to drag his father out during a violent thunderstorm. As he poked and prodded his belligerent father home, the man stopped in the middle of a soccer field and, cursing the heavens, began to relieve himself. A bright and sudden bolt turned his penis into a lightning rod, leaving him coffin-bound and with something resembling a Barbie doll crotch. It also left Van Detta with an all-consuming fear of lightning.

I followed Van Detta as he went house to house panhandling for his and Ralph's bible camp. It took all my skills of persuasion to convince him we could get in and out before any heavenly fireworks, and the odds of him being struck by lightning were less than a billion to one, and, besides, wasn't my money easier than getting doors slammed in his face? He held up, and paused on the cusp of decision.

I still don't know why I'd brought it with me, but from my army jacket I surfaced the tablet I'd purchased from Joe-Bow. 'And I'll throw this in.'

Van's eye lit up.

'128 gigs.'

We were on.

That night, amongst rising winds and a steady drizzle of rain, we took our places. The meeting was for 8, but by 8:30 Joe-Bow still hadn't shown up. I was hiding by a bush on a bicycle path with an incline (the high road?) a perfect vantage point of the meeting place. Peering over I saw Van Detta crouched behind a tree, growing progressively disheveled against the rain.

About 8:40 I heard a crashing through the woods, and Joe-Bow was standing in the clearing, dripping wet and muttering. He began pacing about, his muttering growing louder yet all the more incoherent.

I gave the wave, the signal for Van Detta to advance. It went unheeded. By this point he wasn't just cowering from the weather, Van Detta was on his knees searching the heavens, murmuring some incoherent prayer.

'FUCK – '

I waited for my name to follow Joe's F-cry. When it didn't I knew he'd forgotten it. Fucking typical of his type. I looked back to Van Detta and found him staring at me, eyes a-glass, terror etched across his face.

Lightning cracked down illuminating the woods.

'FUCK! FUCK! FUCKING-FUCK!!!!'

Growing increasingly incensed and increasingly articulate, I knew Joe-Bow wouldn't wait much longer. If he left unhappy I could never go to school again, at least not without facing his elbow and an emergency visit to the dentist.

A thunderous explosion followed by a second bolt of lightning. It struck the horizon of trees, igniting a great maple.

Another cursing outburst and I could see Joe-Bow, eerily backlit by the rising flames, fixing to leave. Again I waved to Van-Detta. He was on his feet, hands undoing his fly. I watched speechless as he pulled his penis from his pants and looking up to the sky, began to urinate.

'Daddy, I'm comin'.'

My speechlessness became Joe-Bow's.

'Daddy, hang on... I'M-A-COMIN' TO YA!'

Joe-Bow turned to leave. It was only then that I understood what was called a 'Hail Mary.' I cried out to Van-Detta, 'The burning bush!'

Van-Detta looked up from his business to the flaming maple. Eyes aglow, he slowly raised his arms towards it. I was up from behind my bush, hair pasted to my face with rain.

'Take heed of the smoted one!' I continued. And yes, my bible quoting is shite, never the less, it brought Van out of his trance and he turned to Joe with biblical focus.

'Smite the smoten!'

Van Detta charged towards Joe.

And then it happened – my phone buzzed.

I'm not particularity proud of this, but like many others when it happens my eyes, not just my eyes, when it buzzes my entire body's attention turns to my phone. As if whoever or whatever is on the other end is somehow the answer to all life's problems. Pathetic.

My eyes should have been on the prize, Van Detta and Joe-Bow but there I was reading a notification, apparently one of vital importance to me and dozens, if not hundreds, of other internet 'friends' of this person who was commenting on a picture of herself; not a new picture but one posted a week previous.

-Forget you ever saw this picture – I'm blonder now!

This was tacked onto a list of her other *need-to-know* annotations:

-Just woke up and there's no hot water!

-I tan on both sides for the same time, but my back's always darker and I can't really see my back. Crap!!!

-It's awful what's happening over there. We should all really do something about it. Right?

Diamonds of wisdom!

Anywho… Van Detta was inches away from contact with Joe-Bow who stood frozen. Bullies it seems are not very good at improvisation, at least not when they're the victims. Leaping off the ground Van Detta threw a soaking elbow straight into Joe's nose. Bone-breakage is a sound unto itself, sometimes bitter, sometimes sweet – for that particular sweetness I felt I might need to balance out with an insulin injection. Joe-Bow collapsed, dropping his bag with the booty and crying out the same articulations as earlier, but this time in pain and fear.

I'd instructed Van Detta once he'd realigned Joe-Bow to grab the booty and fuck-off. Fucking off he wasn't. Placing a boot on Joe's mouth he squeezed his face into the mud, and stared down at him as if to kill. As much as the idea intrigued me, I felt it wasn't the right thing, though funnily enough shattering his face was. Anywho, a clap of thunder shook Van Detta from his focus and he grabbed the booty, rushed past me, and out of the park.

The next day, counting his Bullies Inc. wages, Van Detta informed me he was done. When I pressed him why, he said it was between him and God. Not for a second do I believe in God, or Jesus, or any of them. I'm no atheist, that somehow commits me to the whole religious phenomenon; you know I have to acknowledge a God in order not to believe in a God. Nope, just don't get religion and its fucking litany of rules.

In any case Bullies Inc., now two for two, was without its realigning-torpedo. That's what Murder Inc. called their killers, Torpedoes. Just love that! But without a

Torpedo, Bullies Inc. was just another hollow corporation, much like my bank who's always trolling for new clients with giveaways like a free microwave with any new account over 400$. I'm surprised I haven't seen customer come-ons like:

JESUS SAVES. *At our bank!*

If my bank, if any bank had all the money in the world except its last dollar, it would seek that dollar out and mercilessly hunt it down until it was theirs. In that regard banks have a close affiliation to bullies.

12

AdultHoods and Justification...

With Van Detta gone I found myself at a crossroads. Adults say that, *'I found myself at a crossroads...'* Anywho, with Van Detta retired from action and the local constabulary investigating the matter; like Ralph's, Joe-Bow's parents got involved demanding justice for their precious son, a son they said was not only a model student (I'll concede he had good grades) but a model youth. Oh to see life through the denial-shaded glasses of adulthood.

Have you ever seen a young child in denial? Not me. Little children don't deny, they don't even know what it is to deny. And why would they? They speak or whisper or cry or scream whatever they feel is happening. At least until adults teach them not to.

The same goes for lying. A child tells only the truth until convinced by adults the truth is wrong or unmentionable, and they're likely to be punished for speaking it. 'Just tell Auntie M her new tartan mu-mu is lovely.' One rarely grows out of these defilings, one grows into them, their instincts choked like a snake coiling around its prey, each breath twisting tighter until their victim is unable to draw even the smallest of breaths, or truths.

That same truth-crushing wisdom creates our television ads. You know, cleaning products that speak telepathically or with animated cardboard mouths; zero calorie chips with warnings of anal leakage; toilet paper commercials that make you want to wipe your ass with little kittens; prescription drug ads that spend most of their sixty seconds warning you of the possibilities of side effects: *'Including heart attack, stroke. May result in death.'*

And then adult's grandest innovation, the multi-multi-billion dollar industry that keeps women enslaved and children brainwashed before they are old enough to even speak. Religion. And as the world grows more and more crowded, these Holy ways of living have a way of stepping on each other's toes. Stepping, then stomping. Stomping, then War.

I'm now legally an adult, and have been for some years. Growing up it seemed I wanted that more than life itself, to be an adult, to experience their freedoms and powers and, rather than feel that upper hand on me, feel my own upper hand. Now that I'm here...

Yeah... crossroads. I needed to find a new torpedo, but with Van Detta in full knowledge of what I was doing, this would add another insider, and that doubled my risk of being ratted out. But what's a corporation without some risks, right? What's an ad without condescension? What's a religion without war?

13

Torpedoes be damned...

Van Detta's replacement... It was going to be easy, or fucking impossible. Looking back I blushed at my forwardness in recruiting him; I no longer possessed that naïve chutzpah. No, this time I would move cautiously, prudently, like Nails. I would accept no one from my school; it needed him to be an outsider, someone who wouldn't fall under suspicion as quickly as one so close. Kind of like Murder Inc.; those dudes would bring a Torpedo in from Cleveland to do a hit in Detroit, or Chicago to 'The Big Apple' for similar exterminations. Those must have been the days, you know, before every second Mafia guy ratted out his family then wrote a book about it while his wife paraded her tackiness in her own reality show.

Right about then I was besieged by a tortured case of acne. I'd never been a pizza-face or anything, but this break-out was nastier and angrier than anything I'd ever experienced. Like most my age I'd indulged in salves and creams and lotions to rid myself of the social offences. They worked to a point (but never as efficiently as the animated part of the adds that show the quick and distinct dissolving of said zit) but unless one lives a parallel life, under the exact same conditions, one not using the same salves and creams and lotions, how does one really know if they work? Of course they do—would a drug corporation lie?

Despite my self-consciousness, I felt it best to no longer indulge any acne-warring products. The act seemed one of denial, and I was past any kind of denial. Let the zits fall where they may! And they did. And with the sensitivity of a cold turd, illustrating their *Firm grasp of the obvious* with pointed fingers, the kids at school were astute in their reporting – as if I'd never stepped in front of a fucking mirror – that I had indeed become a pizza-face. And some of those fuckers were the very ones I was protecting!

Anywho... I haven't told you where I got that. Granddad, my father's dad, always used it. 'Anywho, there I was, up to my knees in cow-shit!' (He was raised on a farm.) '*Anywho*, there I was, balls deep in 'er – ' I never understood why Granpy stayed with my grandmother. He died first, which aside from making me sad made me furious it wasn't her. Yeah, I said that. The world's overrun with miserable, wretched people.

I pictured myself chiseling Granpy's tombstone, something light and humorous like him, of course beginning with *Anywho...* But such was not the case. His withered sac of douchebagery wife had something carved on it beginning with: *Our Lord...* How come the people most into that shit seem the least happy?

Anywho, as dad was watching the hockey playoffs, the idea struck me! It seemed weird watching ice hockey with our air-conditioner blasting and mom's first vegetables of summer in bloom... But as dad leapt from his chair swinging rights and lefts, going toe to toe with the brawling ice goons, it hit me.

There was a neighborhood kid who didn't go to my high school. He'd attended my public school, but like all the guys that were: 'Not applying themselves,' he was marginalized into the local trade school. His father, a man whose idea of *Innovation* was a bigger mallet, saw potential in his son's strapping physic and low I.Q. and got him to apply himself to trade-school, ice hockey goonery. This, he excelled at. If I could recruit him my worries of the collapse of Bullies Inc. would be over.

It was a question of how best to approach him. Approaching a lion in a cage you know a chunk of meat is probably all you need. But humans, even goons, can be more complicated. What if he didn't take to the meat, and what the hell would the meat be anyway? What if he'd heard the police were investigating Joe-Bow's broken nose and Ralph's shattered ankle, and put two and two together and turned me in?

I'll call this strapping young man... 86. That's not the number he played under but that's the number he gets. It turned out 86 had heard about Joe-Bow and Ralph, who by then were claiming themselves victims of bullying, but with so much bullying going on 86 couldn't differentiate theirs from others, nor did he care. He needed money for new skates and sticks, etc., and admitted that's why he was on the ice anyway; to wage war on other bullies. His meat was $, our fit a glove...

14

Stones and Sticks...

During my torpedo recruitment phase, I narrowed down my next realignment. I'll call him Will, for it seemed this boy had a will all his own. Bully hardly seemed the right term for him, a true fucking terrorist. And while we're on the subject, what differentiates a bully from a terrorist?

FUCK ALL.

Will's brand of bullying was simple yet effective. He targeted gays or suspected gays, basically anyone he considered gay, and if they weren't already 'out' he'd blackmail them, and if they were 'out' he'd threaten to have them gang raped. No kidding. I never heard he'd actually had it done, but threats of terrorism can be as effective as the actual act; just try getting on a plane.

Will had a great understanding of the fear and shame in name-calling. Adults roll out platitudes like: 'Sticks and stones will break my bones but names will never hurt me.' Really? My dad told me that once, so I called him an asshole – I was grounded for a week! Seems a name; especially names like Faggot, Queer, Cocksucker, names Will liked to use, didn't break bones but they very much broke spirits. Now I know not all instances of bullying are as extreme as the ones I'm describing, but I could only deal with so many and what would be the point of spending my corporation's time on bully small fry? Well 86, my Goon...he actually liked when I called him that, encouraged it in fact, believed calling him a Goon would help him become one. I hoped one day he might see the hazards in that, but for the meantime he was Goon 86.

If he'd been more demure I might have asked him to lure Will into his realignment by playing gay. But asking Goon 86 to do that would have probably had me being realigned. I stressed the appropriate course of action, one that would maintain the tradition created by Van Detta of focusing on the specific body part the bully used in his bullying. Because he was all bluster and bravado, the targeted part would be Will's mouth. Goon 86 didn't understand this, 'What the fuck, a beatin's a beatin'!' I couldn't point directly back to Van Detta and let Goon 86 know about Bullies Inc., but I had to somehow get him with the program of the specific, which I suppose is much like an eye for an eye. The 'Good Book' doesn't say an eye for an arm, a foot for a jaw, a nose for an ass. That publication really knows its stuff, at least about violence and retribution and sodomy and the like. One might say it was ahead of its time.

Once we fostered a plan, next came the $. Despite what it could do for his goonery and how it could hone those proficiencies, Goon 86 wasn't remotely interested in volunteer work (I had to try). It seemed no one possessed the civic-minded spirit I did. Not bragging, but how about doing one for the betterment of the community? Yet I had only myself to blame, once I waved the almighty $ under the nose of Van Detta I'd essentially opened that $ door, one I was never again able to close.

Anywho, during a lengthy debate where he seemed to count the constellation of zits on my face, I was finally able to convince Goon 86 that Will, who used only words on his victims, needed his realignment to happen to his mouth. As luck would have it Goon 86 already had some experience in this department, in one of his ice-hockey dramas he'd broken the jaw of a fellow player; the only hitch – it was with his elbow. I couldn't have it. Van Detta had taken down Joe-Bow that same way and not wanting to repeat myself, at least this early in the game (not to mention setting a pattern the police might link) I asked Goon 86 if there was another way of breaking Will's jaw?

I found myself arguing against his using a hockey stick; too big a clue I figured. In my figuring I was alone: 'I spear 'im with the butt. What's not ta love 'bout that?' Long story short we settled on brass knuckles, which he happened to have. Scary.

Next was where and when. How would we lure Will to some lonely place for his realignment? I couldn't risk Goon 86 tailing him, lurking *inconspicuously* behind Will. That'd be like sending a tank *inconspicuously* after a paperboy. No, this part would be mine, and to tell you the truth I looked forward to it. Me playing, well not so much playing but being a detective after Will and setting the trap.

I've avoided specific descriptions of anyone so far, but Will's simply cries out for one. The bridge of his nose was almost paper thin, and I wondered how any air got through there. Flanking this fin of skin, his beady eyes sat so close together it seemed if he crossed them they might actually touch.

Following him one steamy afternoon, I watched Will meet up with a girl.

Kissy-kissy.

Kissy-touchy.

Kissy-touchy-grabby. Hand-slap!

Lurking behind cars and hedging like some deviant, I wasn't able to get a look at the girl, but pitied anyone naive enough to spend even a second with the creep. So repulsed by the thought I failed to see, until it was too late, that we, the three of us, me staggering to a stop across the street, were at my home! The girl: My older sister!

All those exclamation points! My English teacher Ms. Chong (only when a language is second can someone be so strict) would yell, 'Too many excramation point no good Engrish!' This, despite the fact she lived her hyper-anxious life under a bevy of exclamation points.

Turned out my sister was bringing this fucking asshole home for dinner! It was a kind of Romeo/Juliette thing; Will lived in the house that bordered our backyard, backyards divided by a massive hedge. Years ago, my mother and his mother got into a feud; the same kinda thing children engage in, the same kinda thing adults tell them is immature and childish. Yet somehow when adults do it, winding themselves into reiterating fits of juvenile fury, they are to be accepted with the utmost reverence.

Pre-hedge, my woman's garden and Will's mother's garden bordered against each other and, whenever a weed was found, the discoverer would blame the other for the greenery transgression. This quickly mushroomed into a blood feud. Luckily my dad and the Will's dad had enough sense to abstain from the conflict, and I heard they secretly went halves on a set of thick hedges that now separate our backyards to a height of 16 feet and climbing.

Much the way mom pencil-lined a kitchen wall with measurements of our growth, I used these hedges as measurements of the neighborhood's growth. Like at five and a half feet when the 'Swingers' moved in down the block. Then somewhere around the seven-foot mark, when most of the adults suffered a communal outbreak of chlamydia. And at seven and half feet when the swingers were neighbor-shamed into moving away, leaving behind a trail of divorces that made my dad partner in his firm.

So my sister was bringing this homophobic asshole home for dinner. And I was going to have to sit there and somehow keep my utensils focused on my plate. All through dinner as big sis' was making gooey eyes at him my mind toyed with my phone wanting to call Goon 86 and have him wait around the corner and realign Will on his way home, but something told me not to tie-in the realigning to his dinner visit. That and my phone was charging.

I have to admit Will could really turn on the charm. He impressed my father with his surprisingly astute observations of world news and swooned my mother (she's generally an easy touch, a sucker for pretty much any strapping young man) with little compliments that had her weaving between giggling and drooling. Why couldn't they see it, see him for the fraud and homophobic asshole he was? That almost calls for another, but I don't want to come off as some hysterical abuser of 'excramation' points!

I sat on his every breath waiting for Will to mess up, for some anti-gay remark to slip out where I could point my finger of accusation. The wait proved fruitless. Here's a sampling of the dinner conversation.

Focusing her gooey eyes on my little brother big sis' piped in: 'That's gross! He just spit a bunch of carrots in his napkin!'

Dad grabbed the napkin, opened it and displayed it to the table: 'The court of dinner will note exhibit A: crushed carrots in a soiled...(to mother) honey why are we using Christmas napkins?

Mother: 'We ran out of the other ones. Remember you used them instead of paper towels to sop up that second pitcher of Pina-coladas you dropped on the living room rug.'

Dad: 'I order that last remark stricken from the record. Jury (to Will) you will disregard that remark.'

Mom: 'Well it's true, and next time – '

Dad: 'One more remark from the witness and I will declare this a mistrial!'

Why Will didn't bolt and run from the table I'll never know.

Not being a religious family we don't abide in prayer at the commencement of dinner, but when he's in a good mood, as he was that night, dad will swear in the table.

Dad: 'All rise. Dinner is in session. Those in the family of _____ do you solemnly swear to eat your bounty, all three food groups, until your plates are empty?' This isn't guised so much as a question but a command. Anywho, dinner was far from over.

Dad: 'The court finds the dessert, chocolate mousse and whipped cream not only delicious, but worthy of page 1 in a cookbook.'

Will: 'Sustained!'

Yeah, with that one declaration, 'Sustained!' Will had wormed his way into the graces of my dad, mom, sister and even my little brother. Dad went into his closing argument for the evening, declaring the dinner a success and our guest welcome to come back anytime he wanted.

I excused myself, went to my room and under my sheets imagined all sorts of scenarios.

Will being punched

Will being kicked

Will being punched and kicked

Will being punched and kicked and punched and kicked again

Will drowning

Will burning

Will burning while drowning (fantasies need not adhere to realities)

I heard the front door open and close, listened to Will and my family chirp goodbyes and looking at my clock realized more than an hour had passed with me submerged in fantasy. I decided to go to sleep without washing or brushing my teeth because I felt purged from my imaginings, a soul cleansing if you will, and refused to risk rinsing away of that feeling. Also I was just too tired, my body had actually lived through the scenarios, fists laying out punch after punch, legs driving kick after kick, shoulders tensed from holding Will under the water while hoisting a can of gasoline over his head, arms scorched from holding him under the flaming water. Big sister knocked on my door to do what she always did, tell me about her new guy – gush a more appropriate term – then ask for my opinion of her new suitor. I didn't answer, pretended to be asleep and listened to her move away with an annoying hum and spring in her step that left a knot in my stomach.

I hardly slept that night. When I did manage to doze off I dreamt of Will chasing me with Goon 86's brass knuckles and hockey stick. The next morning I typed out a Bullies Inc. proclamation and then burned it. Written correspondence would be evidence and it was bad business I had Van Detta leave one with Ralph. I had to train Goon 86 to deliver the proclamation in words. No small feat, but it was something for the betterment of Bullies Inc., not to mention an elocution lesson for Goon 86.

15

Bag Fashing...

Look... After you hit him, all you have to say is: *'Leave the Gays alone. Stop Bullying them. Stop Bashing Gays!'*

'Leave the queers alone. An' if ya ever come onta me I'll break yur' spine!'

Teaching a steamroller to do the tango...

Being a pragmatist, I decided I needed to deliver the verbal portion myself. This would put not just Bullies Inc. but myself at risk. Yet in the face of quandary does a good leader not venture into battle and mix into the fray? Probably not so much now, but they once did. I would take a page from those historic leaders.

I would need a disguise. My mind spun through a litany of scenarios before deciding on a pair of my sister's pantyhose pulled down over my head (involving her in her boyfriend's demise left me tingling-glee). As well, I've always found that impalpable quashed-faced look rather scary, at least in the movies, and if nothing else we know the movies are bastions of authenticity.

Goon 86 and I staked out an abandoned parking lot by an abandoned factory, one of Will's routes home. We staked it out knowing he walked it after his baseball games, Captain of the team no less. School was nearly finished and the days were growing long. Night was a must for Will's realignment, and I hoped his game would last long enough so he would have to make his trek home in darkness. We watched the game from a distance, neither cheering or booing. Though I did have to slap a hand over Goon 86's mouth when, after a dicey call, he cried out for the umpire's death, although he referred to him as 'Ref.'

The game played quickly and, being only seven innings, ended shy of darkness. My ragged corporate nerves couldn't take another night of waiting so I hustled Goon 86 off to the abandoned factory's abandoned parking lot where we waited behind its abandoned dumpster; one so ancient and corroded if separated from its rust would look like a jig-saw puzzle. I wish I could say we waited in silence, but we didn't. I began to wonder if Goon 86 was like one of those sharks that have to keep moving to get water through their gills, only with him it was talk. And not the talk that titillates one's intelligence, it was more like... mmmmmn; I would imagine that of a bully, a bully bragging of his conquests. The saving grace to Goon 86's lip-flap, the thing that separated him from a regular bully, was his admitting to having lost as many fights as he'd won. A true bully would never admit that. And he was entirely gracious in complimenting his conquerors! Anywho, just as I was beginning to not hate listening to Goon 86, along came Will.

Chin cocked in bravado (Will had hit two home-runs and knocked in four other runs) it was all I could do to not race out and kick him in the face. You know that feeling? If you don't you've either led a blessed life or live eye-deep in denial.

Will's repulsive strut was fast drawing him upon on us. Looking over to Goon 86, I wondered if the glisten on his lower lip was sweat or anticipatory drool. Willy-boy must have sensed something because he stopped dead and looked around like an animal sensing danger. Goon 86 he stepped out from our hiding place—Fuck, I've failed to mention this but, in our original negotiations, I'd told 86 he must disguise himself for any realignments. He wanted nothing to do with this bit of common sense; he wanted Will or anyone else to know it was him, as it would help promote his Goon reputation. With Herculean effort, I was finally able to convince 86 this was a gateway to prison. Goon insisted on choosing his own and, right out of cliché central, his disguise was a hockey goalie-mask; a been-there-done-that-I've-seen-it-in-every-cheesy-Hollywood-sequel fucking goalie mask! If Bullies Inc. had more corporate sway I'd have punted him from the organization the second I saw him pull the thing from inside his sweat pants (this after telling me he only ever went commando).

I can only imagine what went through Will's mind (and Goon's nostrils) when 86 stepped out from behind the corroded dumpster, donning his goalie-mask and brass knuckles. An uncontrolled voiding of the bowels comes to mind. Will froze so it was impossible to gauge his reaction. I mean froze stiff, his face and body totally unreadable. He reminded me of myself in some dreams, you know the ones where you can't run or move or speak.

Without further ado Goon 86 let out this deep guttural pronouncement:

'STOP FASHING BAGS!'

Stop Fashing Bags? Stop Fashing Ba—OH! Stop Bashing Fags! Seemed our rehearsals had not fully sunk into his leaden skull. My Stop-Bashing-Gays had been strained into his

STOP-FASHING-BAGS!

Will looked entirely perplexed. Before I could offer any clarity, Goon 86 hauled off and clocked Will in the face. He dropped like a sack of potatoes; though I've yet to see an actual sack of potatoes drop. But that's what they say, right? Whoever *they* are.

Leaping into action, I yanked the pantyhose down over my face and ran out to clarify the oral portion of the realignment. But there was no need. No need at all. Spittle hurtling through the opening of the mask, Goon 86 stood over a dazed and terrified Will (couldn't read if he'd gone as far as voiding his bowels but the gaining stain round crotch was a dead giveaway) repeating like a record player skipping over vinyl:

'STOP-BASHING-FAGS!'

'STOP-BASHING-FAGS!'

'STOP-BASHING-FAGS...'

Calling them *Fags* somewhat defeated the purpose of the warning, but I think the essence of the message was loud and clear.

Sadly, Will did not come away with a broken jaw. Having never used brass knuckles, Goon 86 claimed he was thrown not only by their weight, but also by his footwear, having not worn skates. He promised to practice on his home punching-bag until his aim was nothing less than pinpoint. So no broken jaw but Will's cheek was fractured beautifully. And when he finally returned to school his face never seemed quite the same. Perhaps it was remnants of the swelling and bruising, but I saw it more as a permanent change of expression, a permanent shade of realignment. After that Will avoided any gays, suspected of otherwise, as if making eye contact with one might release the HOCKEY-MASKED BRASS-KNUCKLE SPORTING GOON FROM HELL! Will claimed he was struck in the face with a line drive (which was somewhat true) and there was never any mention of what really happened that night.

Initially relieved by this, I soon found it a mixed blessing. Will keeping hush about his realignment would keep Bullies Inc. out of the authorities' radar, but how would anyone learn of my corporation and its realigning of Bully-evils? I couldn't be expected to realign each and every single bully! This sent me into a fit of a depression. Sure I feared the police finding out, and devil knows I'd be punished worse than any bully, but my goal was to put an end or at least greatly reduce all the bullying, and with no spreading of the word deterrent, this would never happen. And even if the authorities learned of Bullies Inc., their fears of vigilante justice would have them keep my enterprise a dirty little secret.

My message needed to get out there. Bullies needed to know someone was onto them, someone who would level them worse than they'd ever leveled their victims. Like Aids; when people learned of its danger condom sales soared or people abstained – behavioral change through knowledge. If Bullies Inc. remained invisible, bullies would continue to thrive.

I thought...

I pondered...

I deliberated...

And finally it struck me!

If the authorities, being either the police or school trusties were not smart enough to see the emerging pattern, things needed to be helped along. I'd leak something to the media, hints and clues, so by adding 2 and 2, one of them could make the 4 story their own, unearthed entirely by their personal investigative genius (remember, you can't spell media without Me). If anyone could make a mountain of a molehill (though I felt what I'd achieved was more than a molehill) it would be the media.

16

Like the guy who was asked, 'Do you abuse drugs?'
'No,' he answered. 'I'm very kind to drugs.'

I found myself growing quicker, more confident and efficient with corporate decision-making. I was becoming a leader, as dad would say. He too sees himself a leader and claims that's why he went into law, to fight the good fight, to make the community and the world a better place. Yeah, I know, he's a lawyer, but you try arguing that with him.

Thing is, not once has he made that statement without justifying it with an anecdote; one of a young man (himself) working his first ever job in a tourist restaurant in Niagara Falls. This particular restaurant specialized in seafood. FRESH SEAFOOD. Entering it, one was greeted by an over-smiling maître d' and a tank of live lobsters. Giant, live lobsters. Once a tourist had pointed out their meal (many flashing photos with the poor creatures) the maître d' would have a busboy pluck it from the tank then run it into the kitchen where, instead of tossing the creature into a pot of boiling water, he would toss it into another tank. In its place a prepackaged frozen lobster in boiling-pouch was dropped into that bubbling water and minutes later dinner was served. Few ever questioned the sizably smaller shellfish. At the end of the night when the doors were locked, the giant lobsters were transported back into the display tank. It's not so much the story, but dad always combining the crustacean-swindle with him becoming a lawyer. WTF?

So the problem became how would I engage the media without giving it all away, without making Bullies Inc. susceptible to a hostile corporate takeover by the authorities? While I contemplated that another bully was presented...oh yeah, shortly after his realignment Will ended his relationship with my sister who as you might guess was heartbroken. Listening to her lover's torment my tongue was practically left forked, teeth biting through its thick gristle to keep from telling her the truth about her beloved Bag-Fashing Will.

To prove I wasn't biased, my next target was of the female persuasion. Though not for reasons of gender, hers cried out for an altogether different type of realignment. This girl was a New Age Bully, not the New Age of wallpaper music, incense and 'ohms'. She hissed electronically leaving her victims in the throes of public mortification, which for teens is its own kind of death. This charmer was a Cyber-Bully.

Now I'm fairly savvy when it comes to computers. I'm not claiming myself a geek, but I reasoned this realignment I could field myself, key-stroke for key-stroke, which would have been great because I'd exhausted my savings and was living allowance to allowance, volunteering for chores I'd always considered loathsome. I see the need for housework, floors, windows, laundry, even cleaning out the garage, but why aren't grass and hedges and weeds allowed to grow free? Why do adults insist that everything, especially children, need be wrestled back and trimmed to fit into 'neat, smart' looking packages? Just because most adults try to fit their lives into 'neat, smart' looking packages why do they feel everyone and everything else should be that way?

Now in the eyes of adult law what I was doing was criminal. But if not discovered, am I a criminal? And if they were to catch me but could not prove my criminality, then in the eyes of adult law I am not a criminal. I'm confused too. Do adults ever make sense? You tell me.

I habitually watch documentary crime shows and in this one episode a woman went to the local police, then the state police and, getting nowhere, moved onto the FBI, claiming she was afraid her ex was going to kill her. All three forces feigned lack of man power and time to investigate. Three days later she went missing, three days after that a massive police search was carried out by no less than 120 officers. All of a sudden they weren't so undermanned? They found her, or what was left of her, then another massive search for her killer who turned out to be – guess who? Her EX! Now how much money and manpower would have been saved if those adults had just listened to her? Adults just don't make any sense. It seems they're more interested in punishment of the criminal than the prevention of crime.

I really do enjoy crime documentaries, though they're not minus fault. Without exception these shows blather on about how the victim was sooooo 'beautiful.' So what, a bland or homely or downright ugly person being murdered isn't a tragedy? 'Nothing to get worked up over this one viewers, the victim had little in the way of looks. There'll be no empty spots on the world's runways.' Whew, for a moment there I thought I might lose some sleep, thank heavens that multiple-raped, hacked to death woman wasn't 'beautiful'! And they're inevitably great people too, these victims, these beauties; lifting the spirits of everyone around them, admired and lionized by anyone that had the blessed honor to come into a shade of contact with them. I'd like to make a show about people killed that weren't so beautiful, or so nice, pricks and assholes and bitches and call it: *Did they deserve it?* At the end people could text in: 'Text 555 if you think they *didn't* deserve it. Or text 666 if you think they *did* deserve it.'

So this bully, this girl, I'll call her Anna Rexic; now I'd considered naming her the C-word, but I know the C-word can really turn people off. Yet I've never used the C-word in describing female anatomy, never called it a C__. Not once. For me both women and men can be C__s because for me C__ describes their actions, their behaviors, and that's what makes them C__s. No discrimination in my corporation. Also the noun can become a verb: 'He really C__ed me!' Or an adjective: 'She's a C__ing bitch!' As versatile as its lacking cousin *fuck*, remember when *fuck* really packed a punch?

So Anna Rexic was cyber-bulling a girl (one TV would no doubt label beautiful and divine) by posting accusations all over the internet as to this girl's sexual orientation, claiming her a whore, gay, into bestial orgies, along with a history of mental illness. Then, making certain the girl was entirely degraded and kicked into the gutter, Anna declared the girl's personal hygiene putrid, hence her addiction to feminine deodorant sprays.

Personally, I couldn't vouch for... let's call her Courtney, vouch for Courtney's sexual preferences be it whore, gay, bestial, her mental illness, her personal hygiene or addictions, but the public attacks on her, there for the entire world to see made me angrier than Ralph and Joe and Will combined.

As I've said I'm pretty good with computers, born of an age where they seem to be part of weaning (the third nipple). I've always enjoyed their intricacies and challenges, but I worried Anna Rexic's realignment called for skills I might not possess. And in all honesty, like any worthy CEO (I realized that was what I was to Bullies Inc., that and any other position you might care to mention right down to water boy) I was afraid the realignment might be traced back to Bullies Inc. So I went about gathering (buying) a fake ID that I passed off in an Internet café, and after creating a fake online profile, got onto the social network page where Anna Rexic launched the majority of her attacks. But just short of launching my own attack, I froze. It seemed too simple, mimicking accusations done to Courtney. Tit-for-tat. Well c__ that! Then another computer-based realignment seared into my brain: porn pictures with Anna Rexic photoshopped into them, inserted so to speak, but again that seemed too simple, and might only gain her social status. What to do?

I was stumped. And in my mounting panic I considered bringing Goon 86 off the bench to straighten

Anna Rexic out with brawn rather than brains, but I declined to contact him believing the pen still mightier than the sword. Stabbing her eyes out with titanium fountain-tip would have really hit the spot. But again, it needed to be by *her* methodology. So while I contemplated my move against Anna Rexic, I contemplated the media and how to get them on board or at least interested, you know: bring them *Into the picture*, but not *Of the picture*.

Leaving a voice message, sending an email or twitter link or any of those things (fake ID or not) could lead them back to me, which would be corporate suicide. No, I needed to lay a trail of breadcrumbs that would lead them to their own and obvious conclusion, but not back to me. I considered sending them an anonymous letter; in the letter I would reveal Anna Rexic's Cyber-Bullying of Courtney... I wonder how long until cyber-bullying becomes one word in the dictionary? Cyberbullying: adjective. Cyberbully: noun. Cyberbullied: verb. Bringing up red lines now, but not so long ago the word Internet would have brought up the same red lines.

An anonymous letter seemed the best way to tip them off to Anna Rexic's. Taken at all seriously this would pique the interest of even the most lethargic journalist. I went to bed determined but woke unquestionably undecided. I arrived at school downhearted, the way a CEO might head into corporate headquarters after a dismal third quarter loss. How could I turn this around?

It wasn't original, yet at the time it seemed the best option. Send a letter, but that eye-catching way kidnappers used to send ransom letters, cutting out words from newspapers and spelling out their demands in different cuts and fonts. Only mine, instead of sending it to the victim's family, would be sent to a media person, a *Journalist* as they refer to themselves, informing them not only of Anna Rexic and her bullying of Courtney, but Anna Rexic's ferocious demise. What journalist worth a dime wouldn't leap into that story? And if they put in print that bullies were being hunted down and grotesquely realigned, certainly most bullies would cease and desist their vileness. So I went about buying up each of our city's newspapers and began composing my communiqué.

17

FONT THE LETTER

*T*ake a letter...

WARNING: _____ (name of reporter).

Anna **Rex**ic *is* **a Vile inhuman** C___ **who's** (alright fuck it, you can see how the kidnapper's lettering looked) well along to bullying a schoolmate, Courtney, into suicide!
(Sure I was reaching with the suicide bit, but I was after all trying to grab attention.)

School authorities have been indifferent, and totally useless in dealing with the matter of bullying. Law enforcement have taken that uselessness to new heights, choosing rather to focus their manpower on more urgent matters, like the eruption of J-walkers and the soliciting of revenue by way of pimping dollars from illegally parked cars.

WELL FUCK THEM ALL! I will take appropriate action against this online bully, and when I've carried out my mission she will no longer exist!

most *truly*: **Dolph**

(Also, I used Anna and Courtney's *real* first names and the return address, our actual high school.)

I followed his column, his Facebook, his twitter feed... Now is that not the gayest of terminologies: tweeting, tweets, tweeted? TWITS! Yeah, I also use the word *gay* for homosexuals, but its original use was for being happy, you know: 'A *gay* old time!' Or *Gay* as in bright or showy. It's owned by no one, and as dexterous as the word C__!

Anywho, there was not a peep about my correspondence. And the goddam thing took me hours to cut out and piece together, syllable by motherfucking syllable! Failing art class, I considered taking it in for grading, but common sense dictated otherwise. So once again I got mucky making another F-graded clay coffee mug; one that would join its legion of brethren in the back of my mother's kitchen cupboard, all untouched. 'Who knows where that clay has been?'

I was more than disappointed. He was a print journalist (I tend to trust them more than their glossy, candy-like on-camera cousins) heading a daily column that seemed truly concerned with the issue of bullying. And he was one of the few reporters I actually believed when he wrote things like: 'Our hearts go out to them.' You know those corny yet mandatory statements adults make when reporting a tragedy. Adults will take an unfelt, heartless condolence over nothing said. To them nothing said is worse than the issue itself.

Had this journalist duped me? Had he not received my correspondence? Had he tossed it away as a crank? I delved into the Internet trying to understand how a journalist might deal with such a thing, and, after some extensive hours, learned nothing, save the issue of bullying was getting harder to cover. *Saturation of the subject* was the term. But how many ransom-style letters – threatening ones no less – had they received? Well right there and then I decided, despite the journalistic apathy, to go ahead with Anna Rexic and send something to that lay-about journalist once I'd completed her realigning.

How best to realign Anna Rexic? With all the hours of attention I'd spent on the media I'd clearly been putting this off. How had I not seen this? Precious time wasted! A feeling I'd failed Bullies Inc. besieged me.

And then it hit! All the brawn I'd been using, all the brute force I'd managed into the realignments, in the future all I need do was harness that higher power, the power all the black belts and mixed marshal artists, all the sharpshooters and war mongers hold no strength against, the power that turns men into mice, the power that tangles one's thoughts into unmanageable knots, the power that has stood the test of time, persisting through the ages like the cockroach, the backbone of religion – *Guilt.*

Trouble was, in order to make someone feel guilt, guilt enough to change their ways, that person needs to have a conscious, they need to be empathetic. Now think about it, of all the types of people in the world who would be less likely to possess empathy, empathy being soil to guilt's seed? Bullies, for if they had the capacity for empathy they wouldn't be bullies.

But guilt was something I'd tuck into my back pocket for later. Because if the day came where Bullies Inc. went down, I would wield the guilt sword against the school system, against the law, and against my parents; you know, find flaws in their parenting I could use as an excuse for what I'd done. Sounds awful but at one time or another all kids play the guilt card. Though it was a weapon I'd never successfully wielded against my father, him being a lawyer and all. If guilt didn't already exist, a lawyer would invent it.

So I was back to where I'd started, how to nail Anna Rexic?

18

That morning when I arrived at work, latte in hand, there was a small crowd gathered in my boss's office. I'd never felt comfortable around my boss when he was holding court. He reminded me too much of my father, a braggart, a man who had ears only for his own voice.

I tried sneaking past, but my boss's secretary waved me over. With all eyes on me, I had little choice but to join them. I could see my boss ogling some paperwork on his desk, those around him charged with laughter. Though having already read it twice, at the bequest of his audience, my boss launched into a third rendition. Through the crunch of shoulders I was able to catch a glimpse of what he was reading from, a very old-fashioned kidnapper-style letter.

They were getting a thrill from it, but none so much as my boss who through tearing eyes carried on reading while trying to contain his laughter. Being the pro he considers himself, he did contain his laughter until reaching the signature, Dolf, where his eruption of guffawing broke up my colleges. I won't go into detail about how I failed to see the humor in the letter, suffice to say I snuck away to my desk.

I was irritated. I felt something in the correspondence. In this age of non-letter writing, in this age of quick-fingered emails, word abbreviations and one-word texts, whoever created the letter must have spent hours on it. It seemed too much trouble to go through for just a hoax. I sensed something more. So that night after everyone had left, I went to the bulletin board where my boss had pinned the letter for everyone to mock, and removed it. I wanted to know who created it, and was there any truth to either the bully or what the creator, Dolf, had promised about this 'Anna Rexic's realignment.'

No one questioned the disappearance of the letter, but for the next week most in the office sent each other insta-messages, every word in a different font, each some kind of bullying threat against the other. I felt embarrassed, both for them and whoever created the letter. And I wondered if its creator had witnessed this, and in fact was serious in their threat, what they might do to my smartass peers?

19

Pills-a-Poppin'...

I'd sent the letter, but still hadn't worked out how to carry out my realignment of Anna Rexic. I'd figured out the perfect assault, one befitting the Bullies Inc. mandate; I would hack into her computer, link her up to a bunch of child-porn sites then inform the police, you know interrupt one of their mindless flesh-appliances during his J-walker crack-down and pass on said information. But getting into her computer was beyond me. Sure I'd gotten into my siblings systems, done some casual perusing through their journals and personal Intel to acquire ammunition for our next and inevitable battle (nothing like tossing out a dark secret to liven up a round) but now I needed help, the help of a professional.

The last days of the school year were upon me, and if I was going to use hacking as an avenue into Anna Rexic, the clock was ticking. Sure I could make it happen during the summer holidays, but how then would I witness Anna's walk-of-shame back to school as an accused pedophile.

Like most bullies Anna surrounded herself with sycophants, but of late I spotted something in the three other Rexics, a waning. Was Ms. Rexic losing her luster? Might I get help from one of her shadow puppets in her realigning? Before I could finish that or any other such thought it happened. News of it blazed through the school. Ms. Rexic's shame stricken victim Courtney had taken an overdose of her mother's tranquillizers.

The news put a pall over the school day and a gloom over the student body. I searched out Anna Rexic – I wanted to see what effect this had on her. Perhaps she was already doing the walk-of-shame through the school corridors and I was missing it! Skipping classes I rummaged around and it was times like this I wished for friends I might ask about Anna's whereabouts. I didn't see Ms. Rexic or her Sycos until first lunch in the cafeteria. They sat picking at their undressed salads as if nothing had happened. It didn't seem possible. I wondered if they hadn't heard about Courtney**?** I'm not against giving someone the benefit of the doubt, you know, empathy. A burst of laughter popped me from my ponder and there she was, Anna Rexic, laughing, miming taking a handful of pills then flopping head down on the table. I wanted to stab her eyes out with her underused plastic salad fork. I honestly did.

And then I felt a shiver of guilt. If I'd just gone ahead with Goon 86 and a quick physical realigning of Anna, maybe this wouldn't have happened. Why did I have to be so rigid in my corporate mandate? Suddenly I was pinioned with guilt. And that guilt quickly turned to helplessness. I felt like a ballerina trying to pirouette on a waterbed.

20

As well as stating the first names of both bully and victim, the letter also named the school where it was all taking place. In case it did turn out to be a hoax, rather than looking an fool, I thought it best to investigate all three area high schools for a general piece on bullying.

At the time I was a Jr. reporter, and needed at least two approvals before setting out on a story. With reaction to the letter being what it was, I knew if I so much as raised the subject I'd be laughed out of the office. I decided to go into it on my own time, stealing hours from the day, and working the office late at night. I approached the two schools not mentioned in the letter and used them as a kind of warm up. Both principals were away at a conference, and I was assured by the vice principals that, yes, their schools had isolated instances of bullying, but they were well under control. And none of it, in their opinion, was newsworthy. Having the laymen tell the professional what's important, what's newsworthy, is always frustrating. At the third school, I got to talk to the principal who was not attending the conference. A conference, I was to learn, on bullying. He sounded just like his vice principal counterparts. 'Everything at my school is well under control.'

I have always suffered a kind of passivity. Not a great attribute for a journalist, but don't many of us find ourselves in situations that reflect the vulnerabilities of our personalities? Deciding I wouldn't give in to it, as I did at the first two schools, I pressed the principal. 'Just saying it's under control, doesn't make it so. Now I know there's more going on at this school than you're talking about.' It just popped out of my mouth, strong words for me, and I worried he'd see the surprise in my expression. But his own surprise superseded mine, and he staggered out the remark, one journalists both despise and hold a certain fondness of, for the simple reason that it keeps the conversation open. 'This is strictly OFF THE RECORD.'

Turned out, the day before, one of his students, a rumored victim of bullying had taken an overdose of pills. The now paled principal assured me the student was fine and in a hospital bed resting 'comfortably.' Resting comfortably?

'What's the student's name?'

'I can't say her suicide attempt was the result of bullying.'

'I asked for a name.' I watched blood surge into his face.

'I can't comment on that either.'

'So it was a female?' He knew he'd said too much.

'Yes.'

'And you think it was a suicide attempt?'

'I can't comment on that. Maybe it was just a mistake.'

'Just a mistake?'

'Some misguided cry for help, I can't really comment.'

'Help from bullying?'

'We do not know the home life of the student. Whether or not suicide runs in the family.'

'Whether or not suicide runs in the family?'

'There could have been many other mitigating circumstances. I really cannot comment.'

'Had the student...did they come to you or their teachers and complain of being bullied?'

'We have many, many students come to us with their problems. If we stopped for every one there would be no time for their education.'

On the verge of reaching into my purse and displaying the letter, the warning, I was seized by sounder judgment. Clearly there was something here. But it wasn't about pointing fingers. I didn't want to publicly hang the principal, or any principal for that matter. They have tough jobs, looking after hundreds, sometimes more than a thousand students is no easy task. Add bullying to their plate? I could see their dilemma, not wanting to delve into their students' family backgrounds, often messy and impossible situations. The parents of the sufferers screaming for justice, the parents of the bullies often defending their children, claiming it's nothing more than kids growing up and finding themselves.

In high school I joined a clique. Until then I'd had only two friends. Part of my initiation into this group of popular girls was dropping those two friends, and I did. Then at the urging of my new besties I completely turned on them, spreading nasty rumors, plastering their lockers with hate letters; I was caught funneling sour milk through a vent into one of their lockers. My parents were summoned. Fully expecting a public dressing down I was shocked to hear my parents go after the principal, blaming her for running such a loose education establishment that pranks, not bullying mind you, but pranks like mine would even have the time to come to fruition! When we got home my father stated, 'Missy (Missy is what he called me when he was angry with me) you get one Get Out Of Jail Card, and that's it kiddo (kiddo is what he called me when everything was good again).

I'd been on both sides of the bully fence and found myself wanting to make up for having been on the bad one.

21

DESOLATION...

Helplessness assaulted me. Helplessness denigrated me, spreading through my mind and body like leprosy. I didn't want to fall back to brute force but I had no idea how to plant something into Anna Rexic's computer. If I had a handful of tranquilizers I'd have tossed them into Anna's diet Tab, but again – not my mandate.

Of course I was still getting no help from the media, those fucks! I didn't expect the letter to pass through his hands and straight onto the front-page headline – I am ,after all, a realist – but absolutely nothing at all?

I became haunted by my choice of letter styles. Why hadn't I just sent an open letter? No cutouts or fancy fonts just plain old English and straight to the point? I'd become just another CEO fuck-up, but there would be no golden parachute for me. No, it would be a straight fall from 80 stories of success and a promise to the cold unforgiving concrete of failure.

I'm ashamed to admit it, but I found myself praying. Yes praying, the final bastion of the despairing. I didn't pray to God or any of his competitors (it's a very God eat God world out there) I just asked for plain old fucking help. And I was answered, but not in a manner I ever thought possible. My prayer was answered by way of a washed-out porn star. That's not a typo – Porn Star! And if that doesn't call for an exclamation point, nothing does.

22

I could have kicked myself! I'd gone into the schools ill-prepared, obtained little information and exposed myself as a reporter chasing yet another story on bullying, the one issue schools are averse to talking about. I needed to search out the victim named in the letter, and find out for myself, was this true, had (I'll use Dolph's pseudonyms) Courtney been bullied into the arms of suicide by this girl Anna Rexic, or was she a totally different Courtney? Or was the entire letter just some prank? My gut told me it was no prank, but my gut is not what goes into my reporting. My boss is always quick to remind me of that. 'If I wanted your gut in reporting, your desk would be covered in butcher's paper.' I needed to find a way to assure the school I was there for an entirely different reason, something more optimistic.

Through a friend who worked for the local school board I was able to obtain an enrolment list of the high school. There were close to nine hundred names, and within those, eleven Courtneys scattered amongst the grades. My friend refused to give me any personal information, I was hoping for some home addresses or phone numbers, but she did give me a list of the school's extra curricular activities in which three Courtneys were enrolled.

Not wanting to draw attention to the named school, I decided to go back to all three and tell the principals I was, instead of doing a story on bullying, interested in doing a more positive take on things and focus on their school's extra-curricular activities. It was weak, but it was all I could think of. I needed to hold onto the fact whoever Dolph was had warned of a suicide attempt, and that is exactly what happened.

23

Who is this Dick?

My dad deals with some pretty rich clients. He doesn't like the term rich, he prefers 'Wealthy' or 'Well-settled.' Well amongst these '*Wealthy*' or '*Well-settled*' are some rich eccentrics. It was one of these eccentrics that lead me and my corporation from the brink of collapse.

Dad had just completed a client's third divorce (he referred to it as his annulment hat-trick). As was their custom they celebrated his unshackling by spending the evening in a very high-end 'gentleman's club,' a more honest description – Strip-joint. Turns out this eccentric wanted, besides dad buying him drinks and lap dances, a small but ardent favor. Amongst his many other ventures this man dabbled in what he referred to as the 'Adult arts' and wanted my dad to meet an 'Adult arts' acquaintance of his. Pockets flush with the man's cash, dad felt he had little choice and scheduled a coffee meeting with the mystery man. Trouble was dad was supposed to take me to a movie that same afternoon; Daddy-Daughter day. My guess it's an idea no doubt gleaned from one of the child-rearing books in his library, the one with the cracked spine.

We always used to go to Hollywood movies, but as they grew more and more fake and hero-ish, I told dad I hated them and he agreed, so now we only see foreign films which I like because they're just about people doing people things – no overblown heroics. But I know dad still watches Hollywood movies at night, after I've gone to bed, like he doesn't want me to know, like he's ashamed or something. Why can't he just be himself? Is that why adults won't let kids be themselves, because they can't?

Rather than cancel our outing, dad told me to come to the coffee shop where he was meeting this man. They were scheduled for 2:30, and so I was to show up at 2:45 'On the dot,' and upon his signal bail him out of the conversation (and if the meeting turned out to be advantageous, it gave him another 45 minutes before our matinee started). Gotta love that adult thinking.

I got there early but rather than sit in the open, and be exposed to dad and his guest, I tucked behind a pillar, where I could remain hidden and, with the slightest shift, the entire shop was mine to spy. It was fairly crowded, writers publicly displaying work on their unwanted novels or screenplays, mothers with oversized baby carriages, requiring one to be a contortionist to negotiate a path to either the counter or the washroom; reaching the fire exit was out of the question. Alone at a small table was a trendily-dressed man I figured to be the recipient of dad's next few moments of attention.

While I waited, I watched. The guy obsessively glanced at his phone (the way people check their phone these days, gripping them in hope that the next series of vibrations will tell them they're wanted or just simply relevant, rudely peeking at them in the middle of conversations, those to me are routine so when I say obsessively I mean OBSESSIVELY) checking and rechecking it as if waiting for some call or email that might allow him to live another day.

From my hidden position I watched dad enter, look around, then do the vertical limbo through the landmine of baby-tanks to that lone obsessive soul. Luck was with me; dad sat with his back to me, so I was free to listen in and watch their exchange. Upon shaking dad's hand the man became animated, he didn't seem to sit in his chair but hover over it, his hands awry and winged like birds at the end of tethers; I dare not think where they might have ended up were they not attached to his wrists. Between the cackling mothers, whining children and hissing espresso machine, I couldn't hear what their conversation was about, but I could see by dad's peering around and rising shoulders things weren't going well. Other than court, my dad's not a very public person, he's also anything but animated, preferring a more subtle and calculated approach to things both mentally and physically. (Rather than leap into putting out a fire, dad's methodical approach to the situation could very well leave him part of it.)

Just around the time dad's tensed shoulders reached his ears, a herd of cackling mothers cleared out and I was finally able to catch snippets of their conversation. The fidgety guy was laying out his entire life history to dad; his troubled upbringing, his computer genius which he used to hack into certain government files that made him the youngest in the country to ever go to jail for computer espionage. He claimed it wasn't espionage; he just did it to show off to, 'This chick I was tryin' ta tap.' Judging by his hyper-dimwittedness, I tended to believe him. He was also proud of his crime, which he proved by showing dad a tattered newspaper clipping of the event of his sentencing. Dad was stealing stiff-necked gazes around the shop, looking for me, but more worried someone might be hearing all this and associating him with the guy. 'Guilt by association' is one of dad's most subscribed terms.

The guy went on sharing some of his prison stories, like the time in the showers he was discovered by another inmate, who noting his extremely large penis, hooked him with an acquaintance on the outside who ran a small but highly profitable pornography business.

It was no accident dad went into divorce law. The correct term is family law, but divorce is what he excels in. I guess it could have been corporate law or whatever the others laws are, but definitely not criminal law. Criminals give my dad nervous sweats. Law breaking of any sort gets him on his civic-minded soapbox; that is unless faced with the criminal himself, then he generally shrinks and keeps his mouth shut. I doubt dad even shoplifted as a kid. So him having to listen to this rather loud ex-con ramble on about computer espionage, prison, porn and a certain measurement of inches, both in length and girth, had him squirming in his skin. This guy...seeing's how he'll become a prominent member of Bullies Inc. I'll have to name him. Mmmmmn... Guy Dick. That's it, Guy-Dick.

Anywho, the long and long of it came down to Guy-Dick asking my father one question. 'So like, I know ya do divorces an' shit and...so like the porn business is really slowed down, like a recession and... It's cause'a all the free shit! Fuckin' Internet is filled with free shit, the amateurs just given' it away fer nothin'! Assholes! So like I need ta' outsource *Big Bloody* (pet name for his penis) to like chicks, women I guess. Ya know, like housewives, like divorced ones, 'cept they gotta have like lotsa cash. And not too old. Don't wanna blow my stones in a wrinkle 'er nothin'.' He stopped there, giving himself time to chuckle at his witticism. 'So like, I know you do tons of divorces an' shit, and you must know a lotta gash with cash. So like...can ya hook me up?'

It was then I heard from somewhere deep down in dad's throat a small utterance, a warble. Sitting up he cleared his throat, readying it for what he likes to call his court-voice. He began to utter my most hated phrase, 'You do not want to have this conversation.' I hate it cause it's him saying *he* does not want to have the conversation, so why put it on me or mom, or even Guy-Dick? Well dad's court-voice was a no-show: '...you do not want to have...' his statement warbled out shy of completion. He sounded like those commercials, you know with someone's beached on the floor and trying to say: 'I've fallen and can't get up' but they're choking on their dentures. Guy-Dick addressed dad's, '...you do not want to have...' with, 'Sure I do,' and picked up dad's untouched Danish and began chowing down on it.

The sweet pastry seemed to further loosen Guy's tongue and with growing animation and alarming loudness he launched into the fact that if it really came down to it, he didn't mind too much if the 'Chicks were old. I was only kiddin' 'bout blowin' my stones in a wrinkle.' More silence followed. Dad was no longer moving and the back of his neck had turned crimson. With rising voice Guy-Dick further lowered his standards, this time to accept 'Fat broads' or 'Porkers.' 'I've blown my stones in a roll or two.' Driven on by a sugar rush from the scarfed Danish and dad's muteness, Guy's standards continued to plummet until he succumbed to a combination of both the elderly and hefty: 'If shove came ta push I guess I'd do old Porkers. As long as they ain't wearin' no diaper, er any shit like that!' His choice of words was impeccable.

The one-sided bartering continued. As dad, who I could only surmise was choking on some kind of help-cry, sat absurdly silent, Guy-Dick continued bartering down his standards, this time to men. It started like this. 'I don't do guys. That's not my shit. I mean I'm okay with it an' stuff. But not for me. No can do. But I guess ya know a lot of divorced dudes too, right?' I could see a twitch rise in my dad, like those annoying ones you get in your eye when you're tired or stressed, but this seemed to twitch along his spine then spasm on into his head.

Guy-Dick didn't seem to notice or care, he just went on telling dad he was no fag but, 'Well I guess if it came to it, ya know, shove ta push... Now I couldn't blow a guy er nothin'. But I guess I could rub one out of him. Like if he's still got his pants on.'

Spasm-Twitch-Twitch-Spasm.

'I guess he could take em down, but just to his ankles, not right off or anything cause that'd be like gay.'

Safe to say by the time he was finished Guy-Dick was blowin' the guy – but the guy 'Hadta wear a cumbag!' Mr. Dick ended his pitch claiming he wasn't just some adult movie star about to fade into oblivion. No. One day his name would be 'The answer to a Jeopardy question!'

I could just picture it. 'I'll take Superstars for 1000 dollars Alex.'

'What man rose above his tortured beginnings to become the superstar of the millennium?'

'Who is Guy-Dick!'

I'd seen my dad drunk only once; under his crooked smile he had an almost cute stagger. That day in the coffee shop he had a different stagger. Weighing up from the table he reeled away in the middle of Guy-Dick's take on anal sex and how, 'If the ancient Greek dudes did it with dudes, and they ran the world an' shit, maybe it wasn't gay?'

Figuring my dad was in no mood to take in a matinee I didn't follow him out or call after him, rather I peeked out from my perch and waded into what remained of the conversation by agreeing with Guy-Dick. That I did not believe for one fraction of a second that the ancient Greek dudes who cooperatively had anal sex with other Greek dudes were even the slightest bit gay. This proved not only an icebreaker but something of a comfort to Guy-Dick who at that moment looked very much in need of a friend. And who better than I, valued readers, to cozy up to such a poor lonely destitute human being? And convicted computer hacker?

24

Revisiting all three schools I was introduced to the two principals who had been away attending the conference on bullying. They, as well as the principal I had spoken to, were relieved I hadn't returned for the touchy subject of bullying. All three opened their doors for me to look into the school's extra curricular activities, which I did. Educational cutbacks left these poorly funded, something all three principals implored I report in my article.

Something that's long in the public knowledge is not news. It might be dressed up to be news, but without at least some new slant, it's nothing. This included the school's extra curricular activities: nothing bad, nothing outstanding, always underfunded and definitely not newsworthy. I wanted the bully story; it was headline-making, and just what I needed to advance myself from Jr. reporter to back-bencher.

The deeper I delved, the deeper I felt a truth to it. I threw more and more hours into researching it, and even took to the mailroom every morning, intercepting the office post, hoping for another of those red envelopes that my boss had received the original letter in. Luck wasn't with me. Neither were office politics.

In my bosses office I was confronted with accusations I hadn't been producing, that my nose for a story seemed well out of joint, maybe even broken. I was offended, nobody there worked harder than I did. But then it seeped in, most of my work; most of my focus and effort was being swallowed up by the bully story. I should have seen it coming; unlike everyone else in the office I was no longer receiving those insta-message threats, the ones mocking Dolph's letter. I was put on a month's probation and told in simple enough English, 'Shape up or ship out!'

25

Out and Down

Perhaps I'd brought up his hacking skills too early in our conversation, but Guy-Dick's abrupt exit from the coffee shop had me chasing him for two pleading blocks. Not until I flashed my ID proving he had just met with my father was I able to get him to stop long enough to suggest we might be able to help each other.

He needed more convincing than mere words could ever manage, so I agreed to buy him a drink. While I sipped a coke he downed five beers with accompanying shots of tequila. And even though I admitted to having been at the next table and listening in on he and my dad's entire conversation, he felt the need to repeat his tragic life history all over again. I felt it boundless and self-serving, and by his third somewhat slurred recounting I found glaring holes in the narrative but thought it best to let them slide.

When he finally stopped blubbering, yeah Guy-Dick teared up and became quite misty about the iniquities of his youth (if dreadful life decisions were knitting, Guy hadn't dropped a stitch) I spelled out my situation hoping to get him riled up about Anna Rexic and all her evils. My story, with no self-serving platitudes or glaring holes, was no match for Guy-Dick's pathological narcissism. 'What's it ta do with me? I want 'nother round?'

Somewhere in his drinking I became Guy-Dick's best and, I sensed, only friend. I strung him along with promises to speak to dad about hooking him up with some woman, or as he referred to them, 'Rich bitches,' and in a matter of hours I'd learned more about sex than in all my years before or since, and much more than I still care to know. Guy wasn't a bad guy, and I held no moral stance against his choice of profession, whatever he wanted was fine by me so long as I didn't have to hear all the slimy details. After telling him this for a third time our conversation petered into painful silence. Crickets.

From the corner of my eye I watched something light across Guy's face and, sitting up, he invited me to an event he seemed suddenly and alarmingly proud of. He wouldn't tell me what it was, but told me to dress up, 'As old as ya can.' I was frightened but, as it was happening in a public forum, I decided to do as he said, attend and 'Dress as old as ya can.'

For a movie premier (at least to my way of thinking) the event seemed lacking and meagerly attended. Housed in the back of a sex shop, the ten guys there came only to meet his five female co-stars who had all cancelled their appearance; the film cunningly titled 'Multiple Blows to the Head.' The fans who came specifically for Guy-Dick seemed some karmic blowback, both the women old and overweight but tickled-pink to see him in person and have their DVDs signed by their master swordsman! Guy was gutted.

My dad always said, 'When someone's down, that's when you can *Get the Best* from them!' I think what he meant in that predatory statement was, *When someone's down, that's when you can wring the most from them!* I couldn't help it; Guy-Dick's pathetic slump turned me into a predator!

I hammered him with Anna Rexic's brutality. When this didn't work, after emptying my pockets on more booze, and under the guise of us copping some good drugs, I managed to drag Guy-Dick to the hospital where we peeked in on Courtney who was in the process of being wheeled to the psych ward for evaluation. It wasn't really Courtney, and I didn't know where the girl on the stretcher was being wheeled, but truth is a tangled road.

The sight had Guy collapsing into a hallway chair, head bowing between his legs. I looked about in fear; Guy had bragged of this, and his two stout fans at the premier begged to see him perform it live; Guy was so dexterous he could actually fellate go-down on himself. Luckily that journey between his legs was only to keep from passing out.

Maybe it was the shock of seeing 'Courtney' rolled off to who knows where, maybe it was my lecturing him on becoming a better person and guilting him for cruising Sex-Anonymous meetings (talk about a predator) or maybe it was my mentioning there was no better chick-magnet than becoming a 'Hero.' You don't have to believe in something to leverage it. Whatever the reason, by the time we hit the street outside the hospital Guy-Dick's fingers were screaming for a keyboard.

26

Local girl arrested in child pornography sting

A local high school girl was arrested
in an ongoing child porn investigation.
Due to her age police cannot reveal
the girl's name. Four charges have
been laid with more to follow.

My boss snatched the story and the headline, and there was nothing I could do about it. I saw no point in continuing, nor did I want to get caught anywhere near 'his' story, I was in enough trouble. It was back to golden anniversaries and centenarians.

But I could feel Dolph's frustration in bullies reigning supreme and unpunished.

27

Gotcha Bitch!

I wish I could tell you how it all came about, how Guy-Dick's computer wizardry merged some god-awful felonious, *For fuck-sakes-reinstate-the-death-penalty!* websites with Anna Rexic's laptop. Safe to say both things hooked-up and the rest is pure poetry. If only I could've heard the *clang* of the cell door closing on her!

Imagining that *clang*, imagining Anna Rexic's tears, I realized not only was I missing out on seeing justice served, I was also missing out on sharing these victories with the victims. And what celebrations they would be, forget the Olympics, dispatching one's enemy is better than any medal; it's its own rebirth, a life renewed and unencumbered by the horrors of being bullied.

And I'm sure Guy-Dick would've loved to be involved in any bully-free festivities, bottle in one hand, joint in the other, brain running wild with multitudinous illusions of grandeur, fantasizing some nubile pounds of flesh as reward for his heroics. Sadly, with her realignment happening so late in the school year I wasn't even able to witness Anna Rexic's return and walk of shame. Tears.

With school closed for summer it became difficult to select Bullies Inc.'s next realignment. In the summer months kids tend to disperse, yanked away on family holidays or sent away to camps. With the herd of victims thinned out, bullies tended to back off and go into a kind of hibernation if you will, leaving them all the more ravenous at the commencement of the new school year. I could not let these months pass bully-unrequited. I was beginning to see why those horrible army generals are always hankering for war – what the hell is a troop to do without an enemy in their sights? Idle hands are the devil's playthings.

In my neighborhood there remained ample evidence of bullying; nervous kids who dropped their eyes like beaten dogs when anyone walked past, less adventurous kids who stuck around their properties peeking past hedges and tree trunks before scuttling out to retrieve a lost ball, bullies transferring their aptitudes from empty schoolyards into their homes and exercising them on younger siblings or pets. I'd promised myself Bullies Inc. would not get involved in any family matters, those were unwinnable. You know, the way a battered wife jumps on the cops as they put her bullying husband in the police cruiser. Just too messy.

Anyhow I needed to find something quick because lazing about the house made me a sitting target; dad was haranguing me to go into the office with him and begin learning the, 'Letter of the law.' Awwww, just one? The thought of immersing myself in such actions was vomitous, as were the multiple and unending invitations to accompany my mother on her various social and charity events (absolutely stereotypical but there you have it). Though I did consider how I might qualify my corporation for one of my mother's charity drives; doesn't charity begin at home and wasn't charity about helping the community? Needless to say my consideration of the matter was fleeting. I was desperate, not stupid.

Then there was Guy-Dick who was in the midst of becoming my very own Frankenstein monster. For his *'Heroic'* act of bravery he demanded, *'Just Desserts!'* (Somewhere in the dark recesses of his mind there lurked a ticker-tape parade and Time magazine's 'Man of the Year' cover.) Entirely broke I had nothing to offer but the, 'Civic pride in having performed the bully-ridding function.' He harangued me about my promise to reconnect him with my dad, 'Cause he's hooked up ta so much rich-bitch-pussy!' (He had a way of turning those three words, two adjectives and a noun, into one single noun: Richbitchpussy.) I'd meant it at the time but the promise had withered to a lie, though I did have passing fancies of bringing Guy-Dick home for dinner, you know seating him next to dear old dad and watching the fun!

I told him these things take time. He said he'd *'Done his Part,'* now he wanted *'His part Done!'* Wordplay not withstanding, Guy-Dick demanded some form of payment, 'Your dad, richbitchpussy, or the cops!' He was just dim enough to do that last one. I informed him any kind of police contact would land him in jail where he would find himself surrounded by unsavory and vengeful men who upon hearing of his kiddie porn connection would gladly, 'Kick the tires and take a Test Drive of Mr. Dick the former porn star (he hated when I referred to his stardom as former) and get *their* parts done. His lips moved slightly as if he were forming the words of what I'd just said and, once he came to the end of my sentence, they stopped, giving way for a rising pale that drained all color from his shoulders neck then face. Even his reddish eye-whites seemed to blanch in the process.

Guy-Dick went into a disconcerting pout that skidded into a distressing mope that entirely ditched itself into a full-blown sulk. I borrowed against my next month of allowances and treated him to a 'Massage.' I waited on the street (Guy-Dick seemed in the kind of headspace I thought it best to keep an eye on him) and upon his exit he was not only smiling, he was laughing. 'Ya shoud'a heard 'er' (I have to admit his Asian accent was spot on) *'Dar-ring, nec time you com 'ere you no drink too much...My-Arm-Get tiiiired!'* It kinda put the whole thing into perspective.

In case you're wondering how I felt about Anna Rexic, of her being arrested for Bullies Inc. planted kiddie porn, of how her high school years would be ruined, and her only chance for an unfettered life would be to move away (though rather ironically is there really any place you can hide from the Internet, Anna Rexic?) if I was at all upset or remorseful of my Bullies Inc. wheeling and dealing on her, the answer was yes. Yes indeed.

Indeed, because I knew in time she'd be cleared of the charges. Police forensics would figure out the cut and paste job that placed all the filth onto her shiny new Mac and she'd be proclaimed innocent, but how would she understand the connection between being a bully, being hacked, and her realignment? My bad. We may have taken another bully off the streets and made the world a better place, but she might never know, and if she didn't, no one else would. I needed the fucking media.

28

Reporters descended on the school and 'Anna Rexic' the kiddy porn girl. But after a couple of crazy days with both the police and Anna Rexic's lawyer refusing further comment beyond what had already been printed, my boss roved off to something new and more glamorous. His shallow departure from the story incited me and I thought fuck him, fuck them all. Turn the other cheek – you bleed a yellow streak. Just go after it. I tracked down the rumored suicide attempt victim, Courtney.

It was Courtney's mother I had to convince to give me an interview. Playing agent to her daughter she'd held out against all media offers, but when the spotlight of attention shifted to Anna Rexic, she was more than ready to talk. Mother made what she termed an, 'Official statement' about her daughter being bullied. For reasons against this case being identified I cannot quote her, but even then her 'Official statement' was generally unquotable, at least for print, radio, or television. Cowering under her mother's severity, I was unable to draw a single word from the girl. I left their house under a cloud of hopelessness. Why hadn't I been able to shift the conversation from mother to Courtney? That was real journalism. Was real journalism beyond me?

At work I hid in the mailroom. Then came another letter, not in kidnapper style but in the same red envelope as the first. And this time the letter was addressed to me.

29

Unacceptably interesting…

In my dream I died. At the funeral service dad took to the pulpit to deliver the eulogy. He didn't have cue cards or anything because being a lawyer dad knows how to memorize speeches and, from the velvet swaddling of the casket, I felt proud he wasn't about to narrate some shite about how I was sooooo beautiful and how I'd lifted the spirits of those around me and was admired and lionized by anyone and everyone that ever had the honor to come in contact with me. At least I hoped he wouldn't. But when he looked out to the audience it was no longer dear old dad, it was me. The audience was entirely made up of kids from my school, hundreds of them, each one texting on their cell phones.

Not exactly what one wants to dream, even in death those around you won't take a minute to pay tribute to your life. Clusters of conversations broke out as to how many bars people were getting on their phones and as people tend to do, everyone started looking in the air. Do you really think you can see cellular signals in the fucking air? Maybe that should have been the epitaph on my tombstone. Five empty bars.

Still demoralized by the dream, I was sitting in a coffee shop (the same one I'd met Guy-Dick) trying piece together what it all meant, but my thoughts kept getting interrupted by two thirty-somethings discussing recent tragedies in their lives. For one the loss of work, the other a crushing tax audit. But the primary piece of conversation I heard coming from both sides of the table was, 'It's all good.'

What a trendy piece of claptrap! Since the term became a conversation cornerstone have any of you heard someone use it where it didn't follow misfortune or catastrophe? Not me. When things are bad why can't people just admit it? Why's it frowned upon to feel bad? Why must we say shit like, 'It's all good' when clearly it's, 'Not-all-fucking-good.'

It's part of adult's new millennium, be politically correct, deny your dark side, It's all good' philosophy. But where would they be, my ex-victims now free from the evils of bullying if I'd looked at their tragedies and said, 'It's all good.' They'd still be terrified vestiges of humanity. But it's all good, every last thing is allll goooood!

'That's Interesting.'

Pronounced: I-n-t-e-r-e-s-t-i-n-g, the word drawn out in hopes of cloaking its deceit. Mindless adults have strained this once powerful word into false lengths and then infected it onto their children who use the term the same way their parents do, to cover a dislike or boredom of something that doesn't remotely interest them. 'Yes that's, I-n-t-e-r-e-s-t-i-n-g.' Why can't people just say, 'I don't like this' or 'This doesn't interest me in the least.'

Anywho, having foregone any effort in getting a summer job, choosing rather to sacrifice my time on corporate affairs, I was thusly dragged into my father's office, chock full of lawyers, where I never once heard the term, 'It's all good.' However they did mercilessly flog the term 'THIS IS UNACCEPTABLE!'

Somewhere in those two weeks of shadowing dad, him constantly bragging about my high marks (yep, straight A's) I found Bullies Inc.'s next realignment. Well not next exactly, I'd found another female bully to dispatch, but was still working on just how to dispatch her. This next mark worked in dad's office, and that office was a world unto itself. Watching those proclamation-spouting, luxuriously garbed, over-manicured, perfume-riddled-adults in action was better than any visit to a zoo. You see the trouble with the zoo is most of the animals, at least whenever I go, seem to be on some kind of behavioral strike, laying sloth like, the most movement from them, their tails flicking away enterprising, un-slothful flies. But there was none of this at my dad's office, they were buzzing flies taking bites out of the corporate money turd then greeding back for seconds, thirds, fourths and fifths. But amongst their immaculate herd, standing out from the rest was a certifiable, one hundred percent grade-A bully.

It had never occurred to me to realign an adult, but of course there would be bullies amongst them. I'll call him Al Kida. Al was a terror against anyone below him on the corporate ladder (if they were actual rungs I'm sure he'd soil his shoes in dog-shit before using them) and to my surprised disgrace no one seemed to notice or perhaps care. I came to the assumption it was because Al Kida was not only a partner in the firm, but its top earner, which in the adult world means carte blanche as far as doling out abuse.

I asked dad why this skirt-chasing, case-stealing wolf-of-a-man was allowed to roam free, but dad just laughed it off and said, 'It's all good.' When I wouldn't let it go, Dad claimed I was reading too much into what he referred to as Al Kida's 'office shenanigans.' I didn't know any 'shenanigans' that left people in tears so I decided to take matters into my own hands, and Al Kida became next up for realigning.

But I would need to come at this in an entirely different manner, one befitting an adult. You see with all his years of terrorism and assholeism I believed a simple beating would not leave the appropriate wounds for any lasting transformation to Al Kida. So I was left to ponder an Interesting, Unacceptable, All good situation.

30

The second red-enveloped letter warned of another bully to be taken down, a girl labeled Bo Leemic; I had to give Dolph kudos for her name branding. This one also made it clear that when my boss didn't take interest in the first letter, and saw I had, I was being handed the torch. It made one thing clear; this person must have seen me in one of the schools I'd been researching. I didn't believe a teacher would go for any vigilante vengeance, sure maybe a school caretaker or something, but that's not what I felt. I sensed it was a student.

Not only did this letter take credit for Anna Rexic's arrest and why, it stated with her out of the way, bullies like Bo Leemic would be next to fall. This letter had the title: BULLIES INC. along with its corporate mandate:

If you fuck me over, there's always a chance we can bury the hatchet. If I accept, there's always a chance that hatchet gets buried in you.

It also took credit for two others; boys from local high schools who led bully lifestyles and were now either on crutches, or sporting a broken face. Both these stories checked out. It could have been anyone tying these incidents together and claiming them as their own, but the whole thing was just too bizarre and the statements too accurate. It also warned that any media manipulation of the facts would make them next to fall. I chose not to share this information, so I would be going into this alone. This both frightened and somewhat thrilled me.

31

Revenge is the new Acceptance

I was floundering. How would I realign an adult, the lawyer Al Kida? What could I do to make him realize the errors of his life? And there was my usual concern, what if I was caught? Dad would probably be disbarred. I thought long and hard (Guy-Dick would love to hear me say that) but no solution presented itself. So I turned my sights to the girl bully who'd recently crawled out from under a neighborhood rock.

I pegged her as Bo Leemic. Her target was my sister. They were working the same restaurant for the summer, both as waitresses and Bo Leemic had taken it upon herself to steal my sister's tips and threaten her out of any extra shifts, this while she was supposed to be training her! I learned none of this from my sister; I weeded it from some excruciatingly dull and foolish entries in her diary. Seemed my sister had some kind of inkling towards sainthood; that she could talk sense to Bo Leemic and wean her from her angry ways and into my sister's healing arms of friendship. My sister... the bully whisperer! She can be such a tool, such a fucking mark. Joan of Mark. I could see her marrying and trying to convert a wife-beater. 'Please it's okay, John just needs more understanding and more love.' Right, understanding, love and perhaps a few more of your teeth embedded in his knuckles. Well I wasn't about to wait for understanding and love to realign Bo Leemic. The question was how and whom would I recruit for the mission?

Thinking it over, unlike my other realignments, I figured this one might be considered an act of vengeance. You know, what you do to my family you do to me. Not the original Bullies Inc. mandate, but think for a moment; a car accident on the freeway. When police arrive they close off lanes, sometimes all lanes causing miles-long gridlock where thousands of cars idle away wasting countless gallons of irreplaceable fossil fuels waiting for whatever the thing up ahead is to get out of the way so they might be on their way; this while the police take countless photos and measurements in order to calculate one thing: who is at fault. Why? So someone can be blamed, be held accountable, so someone can be punished. But it won't bring the human road-kill back to life now, will it?

Billions of $ are spent on trials, not just so the bad person is taken off the street, but for retribution. How many times have you been watching television and seen the family of the victim walk out of the courtroom happy that the guilty party is now going to serve three consecutive life sentences. Adults, how is that even possible?

Traffic tickets, parking tickets, J-walking tickets, fines of all kinds, in part are they not acts of vengeance? So the *Unacceptable* is made *Acceptable* by rifling money from our wallets! Right. So where's all this leading? Occasionally I suffer the odd twinge of guilt for my participation in Bullies Inc. and these little diatribes help to sort me out and keep me on track. It's as simple as that. Revenge is the new acceptance!

I couldn't go to Guy-Dick for help as I was still avoiding him and his demands for 'Pussy' payment. As far as my other former cohorts were concerned Van Detta was retired to the bible and Goon 86 was at summer (goonery) hockey camp. What to do?

The restaurant Bo and my sister worked in was situated at a local mall. As I strolled its thruways I stopped to watch a group of teens that seemingly had nothing better to do than hassle girls and old people. I edged onto one of those mall benches, you know the backless ones with the heavily shellacked inflexible wooden slats that seem to say, This isn't very comfortable, better get up and buy something! This one was crowded with old men who while clutching canes and walkers watched the teens with wary eyes, commenting on them like football announcers do every Sunday afternoon, except these guys whispered like golf announcers. (Why do they whisper when they're nowhere in sight of the golfers?) They sized up each teen for strength and toughness and fight-ability – as if any one of them was about to get up and take one on. One of these old guys didn't talk as much as the others, he seemed more with the teens, you know whenever they pushed or began wrestling each other he was right there, his frail body bending, twisting, cracking to their every move.

After a while the teens sashayed off. Once they were out of sight the old guys got up and heading in the opposite direction congratulated each other on how they'd chased them off. They left that one guy who was going toe to toe with the teens. Soon after this little boy ran out of the mall daycare and came to him crying. Call me a snoop, but it was heartbreakingly awesome. The little boy was crying to his grandfather saying, 'They wouldn't let me play with them. They said I can't do what the big boys can do.' Well that old man looked back to where the teens had been, and he too started crying.

I realized I lived in that golden age between them, not too young and not too frail, the active age where leaders are born. I would take up arms against Bo Leemic *myself!* I would forge the realignment *myself.* And I, *myself*, would become all of Bullies Inc.!

I didn't encompass the brawn of either Van Detta or Goon 86 nor the computer savagery of Guy-Dick, so those avenues were out. I would have to find a level playing field for myself and Bo Leemic; one where I could wholly realign her and be able to deliver with frightening clarity the Bullies Inc. message against any future terrorism.

I found out when her next shift was, one where my sister would not be in the restaurant (her dullard diary was a goldmine of information) and settled in for an afternoon of planning the first phase of it.

32

With school out for the summer it became more than problematic to track down this new, intended victim. Having only an alias didn't help. I wasn't about to start asking around the community, 'Do you happen to know someone who might fit the description of being a bully, and labeled Bo Leemic?' Not exactly sleuth reporting. With staff probation hanging heavily over my head I should have just gone about my regular business and hoped for a break in the case. But that kind of passivity would get me nowhere.

I decided to go back to see Courtney, but this time speak to her alone, without being under the smother of her mother. From a restaurant patio on the corner I watched their house. Again, Courtney's mother stuck to her daughter like the secret service on President's day. Watched over her while she cut the lawn and trimmed the hedges. Wouldn't even let her answer the door unsupervised. It took some time, but judging by the way she kept looking back, when Courtney did finally manage to leave I don't believe she just left the house, she escaped her mother.

I tracked her to a local mall and followed her to a restaurant. Inside she slipped into a corner booth. Then, as if worried of being followed, she looked around, straight towards me. I froze. She looked not so much at me, but past me, as if I wasn't there. It was clear she didn't recognize me. While I nursed a weak cup of coffee, trying to figure the best way to approach her, a young waitress sat down and started up a conversation with Courtney. I couldn't hear them, but they clearly knew each other and whatever they talked about looked intense. But then again a misplaced tube of lip balm can make teens exhaustively intense. Then Courtney broke down. The waitress handed her some napkins and held her hand. It seemed this victim of bullying had a friend, which was a good thing. And watching them I wondered, do I keep after Courtney, or just leave her in peace and move on to Bo Leemic?

33

FTW!

I couldn't believe it, victim and bully together, well not the bully of the actual victim, Anna Rexic was Courtney's bully, but there was Courtney being all friendly with Bo *fuck-the-what* Leemic! Like watching enemy species co-mingle, a mongoose and a cobra buddying up to each other on the couch watching a Rachel McAdams movie. It was my second visit to the eatery, reconnaissance, there to gather Intel on Bo, and she was talking to Courtney like they were besties!

My coffee was all that kept me from totally freaking out. I'm one of those curiosities that stimulants like caffeine tend to doze me up. So, while trying to sip myself from imploding, I wondered if maybe Courtney didn't know about Bo Leemic and her bullying of my sister, and who knows whom else? And maybe Bo Leemic wasn't a full time bully; maybe she just hated my sister. I'd been gripped by that very same sentiment.

Just as the caffeine was beginning to win me over I spotted the reporter! The one I'd sent my second letter to, the one I'd first recognized from snooping around our school. Seeing how my first choice of reporter turned out to be an entirely useless douche, I'd sent my next letter to this woman. But how could she know who

Bo Leemic was if I hadn't exposed her real name? Was she following me? Did she know who I was?

Right about then Bo and Courtney got up from the table, walked out into the mall, and there some exchange was made. At the time I figured drugs, a bully selling drugs, an abused teen buying them, made sense all around. While I watched the exchange from one window, I looked over to find the reporter at another window watching them too! And then I passed out...

34

Hey Dolph, whatcha thinking with that needle in your vein?

They called World War 1 the Great War, but if it was so great then why'd they have another? Or was it so great they had to oblige a sequel: WW2, THIS TIME IT'S BIBLICAL! In the hospital, waiting for my test results, deliberations like these are all that kept me from going completely out of my skull with boredom.

The deliberations also kept me from wondering things like, how many people have died in these starched-sharp hospital sheets? And what about the concrete-like mattress, it must have played host to dozens if not hundreds of urine parties, fecal blowouts and scores of passing lives.

My roving mind drifted from sullied sheets to the reporter. Was she onto me, or just onto the story? Was she waiting for my next move before bringing down the local constabulary? What was in that IV drip leading into my vein? What kind of drugs? Or was it – adult's think they're so smart – a placebo? And if they're so damned smart why do they constantly go after each other's throats?

Well now that I've started... Don't many adult groups, particularly minority groups, do that, go after each other's throats? Women are often virtual c__s to each other in the workplace, gays frequently turn on each other citing the other as being toooo gay or not gay enough, black gangs warring black gangs, white businessmen screwing each other out of money and property like the whole thing's just some fucking board game!

My hospital stay was not as dire as my deliberations. I get these attacks every so often, then a series of tests, then they tell me to watch what I eat, take my medication, and I'll be, 'As good as New!' Thing is they never knew me when I was new.

35

Tribulations and Trials

The day after my release dad took me to one of his most beloved of institutions, Court. He felt an eye on vocation would help my convalescence, you know with the possibility of me becoming a lawyer and all, at least that's what was fixed in dad's mind. In any case he felt it necessary I experience first-hand court proceedings in all their glory. I whined a blue streak not wanting to go; the least he could have done was haul me there during the school year where it would give me a break from that mind-numbing institution.

The room was hardly packed which was good, for I feared finding myself nuzzled between some scabby hooker and child molester. Dad and I sat off by ourselves, the wooden bench whining our presence to the den of unfortunates. Dad began an expertly whispered play-by-play of how the court worked. I'd never known him to whisper, he was always at us to speak clearly and stridently as if every word uttered were to a room full of jurors or some supreme-court judge. Adults say we should never judge, then they go paying hundreds of millions of taxpayers $ to people to not only do that very thing, judge, but bestow them with great prestige in doing so. And while I'm on it, why are judges always so old? I mean, I'd rather be judged by a peer, someone born in or at least close to this century. But apparently older people are smarter and wiser than youth, just look at the state of things.

Anywho, upon announcement of the judge, dad halted all commentary. Within those hallowed walls he took on a kind of persona, heels together, shoulders squared to the bench, jaw righted as if he were about to be minted for a coin. And then it began, one after the other the defendants were called up, each charged with public indecency. Seemed these men, businessmen, were targets in a police sting, all arrested for having sex in the men's washroom at a popular downtown department store. Classy.

Despite the similarity in attire with their lawyers, designer suits and ties, it was easy to pick out the accused; they were the ones with drooped shoulders and downcast eyes, taking their punishment with a heavy sigh and a lightly muttered: '...thank-you your honor.' Now who thanks someone for zinging them with a big fine and ordering them into months of counseling? Dear old dad kept stealing glances at me while grumbling this was really not the norm. The last member of the buggery-bunch, number five, a short, thin but widely framed man stood in front of the judge shamed over like an old fly swatter, while dad sat ridged, bracing himself against any further smutterings. Things were only about to get better.

The next case starred a rather old, sorry looking couple, the woman charging her husband of thirty-seven years with rape. While being sworn in and asked to raise her right hand, she raised her left. Twice. On the stand she pointed a gnarly finger towards her husband, equally gnarly and grubby, and claimed he had raped her on the morning of the...whatever, and wanted him put away so he might go to prison and, 'Understand!' Both were career welfare cases (with a keen eye dad suggested third generation pedigree) as well as what looked like career alcoholics.

The prosecutor started in with the woman asking her name, age, 64 (going on 94) then asked her about the morning of the incident. 'We got up an' had some beers.'

I'm not kidding. She actually said that! The prosecutor half shook his head and asked her what happened next? 'En we had some pickled eggs an' whiskey.' By this time the husband's public-defendant lawyer was sitting back like he'd just won the lottery. As the woman babbled on about their eatin' and drinkin' her dentures came unglued. So every third or fourth word out of her mouth you'd hear this, *Clack!*

Right then I, *'Clack!'* wanted to apologize to dear old dad, *'Clack!'* for making such a fuss over coming. But before I could the prosecutor fired off his next question. 'In your statement you said the defendant started to touch you inappropriately, can you tell the court where that was?'

Like when a dark cloud blackens the sun, all light drained from her face.

'Where's wha'?'

'Where did he touch you? On your body?'

'Where'd –' *Clack.* 'Body –' *Clack!*

Fingers realigning her unruly dentures the woman was looking more bewildered by the second.

'Yes. On your body.'

Clack! 'I er...a...' *Clack!*

The judge called a short recess so the woman could re-paste her teeth. It was awesome. Heaving breaths, dad suggested I'd seen enough. 'No,' I cried, 'NO!' He sat back muttering, 'These goddamn white-trash welfare cases do nothing but cost the taxpayers, of which they are not contributors, valuable court money!' I wanted to add, 'But they more than make up for it in entertainment value!' However Dad was already agitated, I needn't badger the witness.

Complainant back on the stand, I could see pink denture-glue around the corners of her mouth and clinging to her old-lady moustache like little drunken stalactites. She looked around as if seeing everyone for the first time, all the people in the stands, all the security people, the stenographer and the judge. And just when you thought someone couldn't get any more bewildered, the prosecutor again asks her, 'Please tell the court, where your husband began touching you.'

'Ya mean where Jimmy sterted touchin' me?' *Clack!*

'Yes, your husband, James.'

'He sittin' right over there –'

'Yes we know. You've already identified him to the court.'

'To who?' *Clack!*

'Please, just tell the court where he placed his hand.'

'Well –' *Clack!* ''E took 'is hand an –' *Clack!*

The woman stopped. She sat back. All you could hear was mouth breathing, hers, and smoker's phlegm rattling around a chest like a dying motor, her husband's. The prosecutor reiterated, '*Please*, just answer the question.'

She opened her mouth, *Clack!*, then sat up and leaned towards the prosecutor. He edged closer. She whispered something to him. At first I thought what she said drove him away like some big dramatic revelation on TV, but I could see by his watering eyes it must have been her breath. Back behind his desk the prosecutor, who was clearly pissed with the whole thing says, 'I'll not ask again. Tell the court. Where-did-your-husband-put-his-hand-on-you?'

Again she looked around. Then she looked up, as if the answer to the question might be lodged in one of the ceiling tiles.

'For the last time, WHERE DID HE TOUCH YOU?'

A look came over her face, the look a kid gets when the teacher asks a question they're not ready for, and then the whole class stares at them, waiting for them to answer, and the kid sits there stewing between a sweat and a shit.

'Last time—where did he touch you!'

And finally: 'Er...a... What's the fancy werd fer cunt?'

Dad rushed me from the court before I could hear the answer to her question. Funny thing, the events of that morning inspired me to say the words dad had so wanted to hear, 'Maybe I do want to become a lawyer.' In his curt way that slams the door on a subject dad answered, 'There's no need to rush into anything.'

Thinking back on my time in that hallowed of adult institutions, and all the talk of public-buggery, communal-fellatio, and the 'fancy word fer cunt,' it made me think back a couple of years to when dad, after losing a coin-toss with my mother, was left to explain the facts of life. Sitting across the kitchen table from him (mom had taken my siblings to a double bill figuring it might take him that long) I watched dad's hands grinding together. Just above that grating torment, I watched sweat beading across his upper lip and I thought to ask, 'Dad, that moisture on your lip, is it sex-talk pre-cum? Is your mouth getting ready to take the penetration of sex talk?'

At one point, I was going to interrupt him, let him off the hook so to speak with some of the knowledge I'd already gleaned. Even play a little Jeopardy with him.

A man having an orgasm on a woman's neck? Dad, what is a *Pearl necklace.*

A man having an orgasm on a woman's face? Dad, what is a *Facial.*

Don't parents realize they can't come close to teaching what the Internet has already instilled in us? Not just in words but pictures, trillions of them, and video, now in HD! All courtesy of their fellow adults. But I couldn't bear dad thinking he was late or lax in his parental duty so I sat stoically while he stumbled along, me filling in the gaping blanks. Afterwards we celebrated, me with a bowl of ice cream, him with a tumbler of Scotch. Then somewhere during my second bowl and his second tumbler he told me how he and my mom had really met.

The story was they'd met in College, which remained true, but dad went into detail telling me he'd had his eye on mom for quite awhile but couldn't find a way in, as in too afraid to ask her out. One weekend many of the students took part in a ground search, police were certain a girl had been murdered and dumped in the woods not far from the college. Dad had little interest in the search, but followed mom into the mêlée, and as they combed the woods he edged closer and closer until beside my mom he stepped on her toes, dad's such a smoothie, and a conversation broke out, one that led to matrimony. The body was found that afternoon and dad still displays a picture of he and mom posed with a rather bewildered looking county coroner.

Anywho just as dad was dragging me from court, I got a call from Guy-Dick. Seems he had no one else to use his one phone call on.

36

The police traced the child porn on Anna Rexic's computer to a hacker, one who seemed the most unlikely of suspects, a struggling porn star (again I'll defer all labeling to my co-author) Guy-Dick. Upon interrogation Guy-Dick confessed to the crime, yet claimed it was done for a greater good. He stated Anna Rexic was a known bully school authorities refused to do anything about, and her bullying had sent a young girl into a suicide attempt and into a hospital, 'Loony ward.' So he took matters into his own hands and linked her computer to a child porn site.

The police thought him a liar; his bizarre story just a way to validate his crime. But finding no child porn on his computer he could only be charged with invasion of privacy, cyber fraud, harassment, and freed on two thousand dollars bail. There quickly formed a lineup of reporters for Guy-Dick. He claimed his Robin Hood-esque action had landed him in jail, and would not grant an interview without some kind of fee. Basking in the glare of attention Guy-Dick started the bidding at, oddly, two thousand dollars.

Unwilling to be held ransom, reporters created their own stories based on information the police had released. Guy-Dick plummeted off the news charts, much like his porn star career had. I know that sounds nasty, but that's how I went about approaching him; I didn't mention his arrest, rather I told him I wanted to interview him about his career as an adult film star.

I found Guy-Dick similar to many other celebrity types, once he realized the subject was himself, his floodgates opened. He spoke of the tragedy of his childhood, his misguided youth as a computer hacker, and then his not so misguided adulthood of being a porn star. He pronounced porn as if in small letters, and STAR as if in capitals, 'porn STAR.' Without stopping for breath he went on describing the horrors of the industry's dependence on artificial stimulants like Viagra. I would never have pegged anyone in the industry for such puritanism, but there you go. Guy-Dick was a porn puritan.

He revealed the mindboggling numbers of women he'd slept with, but not in the way of conquest. Rather, he saw himself as having touched these women's lives in ways he believed no one else ever could. Each woman not only got to take him in physically (inches and girth were stressed) but they got to take in his humanity and all his other virtues. Clearly it was a man painting a self-portrait meant to halo rather than expose. Having already been cornered into picking up the bar tab I let him go on. And on.

Once I thought him thoroughly lubricated, I turned the subject over to his recent Robin-Hood-esque behavior on the computer. His expression became one of remorse, as if I'd drenched up some personal secret no one in the world knew but him. He went into a story of a teen, one who had manipulated him into his act of unselfish heroism. The teen had also promised him rewards for his heroism, rewards he was rather vague about, but had reneged on. Guy-Dick claimed life had once again swindled him. He then broke into tears.

Weeping, he railed on about being taken advantage of. I was able to piece together the teen was likely the same person who had sent the first ransom letter warning of Anna Rexic's demise, and the second one to me, warning of Bo Leemic's realignment. I began to press Guy-Dick on who this person was, and just as it looked like he was about to answer me, he fell off the stool chasing a shower of his own vomit.

37

Suck an Egg

I saw this thing, a cooking trick where they took an empty plastic water bottle, scrunched it up, placed it over a cracked egg, let it unscrunch, and up went the yolk, just the yolk. It made me think about bully mothers and how I wished they could do the same to their vile offspring. You know suction the bad part back inside and re-gestate them into kinder more empathetic kids.

Yeah... Clearly I was stuck. All my bravado in promising to realign Bo Leemic myself had faded. I was unable to invent a suitable method, or any method for that matter. She continued to bully my sister for tips, for hours and no doubt for kicks, but be extremely nice to me. Gathering Intel on Bo whenever my sister wasn't working, I'd become somewhat of a regular in the restaurant. And with my sister taking her on as a cause, you know, 'How might I convert this misguided lamb?' typ'a shit (preparing herself for Sainthood?) I looked back to the other target.

Accompanying dad into the office three days a week I'd garnered more Intel on Al Kida. Besides being a corporate/office terrorist, he was an immoral womanizer and rumored to have plowed his way through most of the secretary pool; those who hadn't been tilled waited for it like next-numbers at the butcher's. Whatever, I mean whatever as a married adult, but he had three young children! Why is it life's biggest assholes forever insist on breeding? And if all this wasn't enough, I'd also learned it was Al Kida who incorporated the pompous inter-office dialogue that made me want to yank out my ears.

'Let's have a stand-up.' Sit-down to a meeting

'Scope-document.' Read something

'Point of contact.' First talking to someone about a subject

'Deep-dive.' Look into something.

'Drill-down.' Look deeper into something

'Do you have the bandwidth?' Do you have the time?

Even if he wasn't a bully, Al-fucking-Kida needed to pay for this terrible-fucking-pretentiousness! I'd gleaned Intel on him through stealth observance and inner office gossip. I've never been much into gossip, but one morning while I was in the washroom hidden away behind a stall door two of the office secretaries (both in tears) shared woes of Al Kida, and this is where

I learned of his extra marital activities. From then on, after fashioning a very legit looking, *Out of Order* sign I placed on the stall, I proceeded my spying undisturbed and never grew tired from all I heard. And I thought teens were horrible gossips! But then again where do they learn that vile skill, but from adults?

Oh yeah, when Guy-Dick called me from jail in near hysterics, he blamed his entire predicament on me, and threatened to reveal me to the police. I thusly informed him that if he did, if he admitted to sharing kiddie porn with an under-aged teen, that being moi, where did he think that would leave him with the police and their nightsticks? His answer was to hang up. I'd hoped that'd be the last from him, but hope is no one's to command. Yet it was not Mr. Dick reconnecting and wanting a stand-up or point of contact with myself, it was I needing bandwidth to open a dialogue so I could deep dive and drill down into my predicament.

Reconnaissance on Al Kida led me to a certain drinking establishment, I'll call it *Eve-Ills*. Peering through the establishment's front window like some backdoor pervert I forever lost track of him in the crowd, not to mention being asked on more than one occasion what exactly I was doing leaving my breath print on the glass. I needed inside his nauseous world. Now I'd been able to sneak into a couple of bars with Guy-Dick but without him or someone older, gaining access to *Eve-Ills* would be impossible. Hence the need to have a stand-up with him, coupled with a deep-dive, and we entered into a point of contact.

Negotiating with someone in the middle of a nasty sulk is never easy. I've played that part on others with gloriously exasperating results, but the other side of that coin was awful. Between my pleas and offers of money, not a lot of money but money just the same, I imagined all sorts of action-items I could do to his sullen face, all gathered from my addiction to watching cage fighting.

Moping to the bar's washroom I stumbled upon inspiration. But not in a way I would have ever expected. If you had asked asked me, 'Dolf, have or would you ever be inspired by shit-house writings?' I'd have told you in no uncertain terms, 'I do not possess the bandwidth for such a thing.' I mean who the hell reads that shit! Nevertheless, sitting there, prisoner of my body, I could not avoid the prose that filled the back of that metal door, less than a foot away and directly at eye-level (no mistake on the author's part). I wish I could say I'm paraphrasing but the words, by the time I'd reached that last exclamation mark, were permanently etched in my mind. And here are those very words…

Hey moron. Yeah you, fuck!
How do you think you look right now?
Yeah right now, with that long stinking shit hanging out your fat filthy asshole?
You're no fucking Rock Star now are you?
No.
So that being the case, why don't you take that shit-spewing waste-of-flesh corpse of yours, along with your insipid mind for reading this, and do the world a big favor by flushing yourself down the porcelain highway!

Had a sentiment ever been so clearly worded? Had I ever thought the same of someone? I don't mean all the gross stuff, but wanting someone to pull the plug for the betterment of the world? Yes. Yes indeed. Could this be the musing of a kindred spirit? That answer, too, was yes, yes indeed a kindred spirit! I high footed from the washroom past Guy-Dick and his sullen smirk and out the door.

Then who do you suppose needed whom? He followed me down the busy block asking what was wrong and when I didn't answer he began to beg. And just like that shit-house-poet had done to me, I leveled him with a mixture of truth and harshness to the effect of, 'What would I need with a washed-up porn star?' And just for the record Guy-Dick was never a star, he had some leading roles in some third rate porn films where you barely even saw his face. That does not a star make.

Once I saw Guy-Dick crumbling and ready to pull that old toilet handle I stopped and razed him with an ultimatum, Quit acting like a sullen child (I had to explain the word sullen) and accompany me to the bar *Eve-Ills* for some bully control, no computers involved, and not only would I pick up the night's tab, but I would agree to be a character witness at his trial. Poor Dick hadn't thought as far as a trial, and his face dropped like a plummeting turd. But just before it landed there was a split second, one that reminded me of when I was little and our parents took us camping and using the outhouse, once you pinched one off, the moment of suspension before you heard it land atop its fallen colleagues.

I made arrangements for Guy-Dick and I to attend *Eve-Ills* on a night Al Kida would not be there, and put my realignment into action.

38

Guy-Dick vowed never to speak to me again. That day in the bar, through a third heave of vomit, he declared, 'The media makes me puke!' It was difficult to argue against such commitment. Though I suspect it was really because I refused to pay him for his story. But before he so adeptly ended the interview, he'd slurred enough about this teen, this master manipulator, making her sound like some Jr. Svengali, that I decided to turn all attention on her.

Again, with school out it would be a struggle against chance to find her. Where does one hang out to track down a teenager free from school? The park, the local mall? And then my mind winged back to the girl I'd seen in the mall, in the restaurant, the one who was also watching Courtney and the waitress. The one who had fainted and was taken away in an ambulance. Was she watching them in preparation for another 'realignment?' Could she be the Svengali?

39

Throwing Wind to the Caution

If I could reveal Al Kida to his Eve-Ills acquaintances as a home wrecker in the midst of tearing his family to pieces, inspire some empathy, and piggyback this back to his wife who, if shocked and angry enough, would take the kids, divorce him for adultery, then demand the house and most of his salary (dad had always been a goldmine of information), I would accomplish more than any previous realignment! And who knows, dad might even score some work from the deal. Solid corporate thinking if there ever was any.

I borrowed one of my mother's dresses, one she felt too old to wear anymore. Its severe plainness aged me perfectly. Needing to keep a low profile I'd warned Guy-Dick about his attire, as in nothing flashy or loud. So what do you suppose he shows up in? A fucking cream colored boiler suit! You know those one-piece things, a cross between a mechanic's outfit and prison jumpsuit; he had all the style sense of a fanny pack. Dick claimed he was overhauling his image and wanted to come off as less suave (apparently he'd always been haunted by suaveness) and harder, more 'Industrial.'

So with Guy-Dick fully *industrialized*, and me scolding my dress down from the winds we stepped inside Eve-Ills. Truth be known, I was scared. I'd never gotten a really good look inside, my breathy view through the window usually blocked by a succession of lard asses. Looking about the place I was almost disappointed in its ordinariness; it looked like a typical Hollywood middle-of-the-road bar, fake wood, fake brass, fake adults. I reached out for Guy-Dick, but just as I made contact he moseyed from my clutching hand towards the first twenty-something his eyes traversed. And there I was alone in a room full of booze imbibing adults I knew nothing about.

People began watching me. Staring at me. I felt naked. I had no drink to busy myself with; you know, something to stare down into and not come back up until all attention had shifted elsewhere. I looked for him, but Guy-Dick had been enveloped within the sweaty assemblage. Maybe he was already on his way to the washroom with the twenty-something; he'd bragged about such conquests. 'Destination: Washroom. Time factor? The right chick – 2 to 3 minutes!' I hoped for the sake of the woman 2 to 3 minutes meant the time getting her into the washroom and not the time once engaged. There – Before I started all this that thought would never have occurred to me. It was a black-armband day for my youth.

I don't how long I'd been standing there. 2 to 3 minutes? 2 to 3 hours? Time ceased to exist with the rubberneckers trying to stare me down into some malleable pulp. And they did. Or was I already malleable pulp? My mouth grew so dry my tongue became a diving-rod searching for a blink of moisture. I'd never been so out of my element. In that room there must have been 50 to 60 adults, and I realized I'd always avoided rooms full of adults. And then I realized I'd always avoided rooms full of younger people. And then I realized I'd pretty much always avoided people.

Before I entirely shrank or was suddenly carded for appearing my wide-eyed age, I needed to make a play. Bust some adult move. Blend. Mingle. But I continued to shrink and actually began to cry. I was hopelessly out of my depth. What did I think I was doing there, that I was somehow going to make a strike for righteousness against not only a high-powered lawyer, but also a partner in a semi-prestigious law firm? A firm who employed my dad! Risk my family's income for reprisal against someone I never even knew? Who the fuck was I to...

Once again those fucking crossroads. Stay and attempt to carry on the Bullies Inc. mandate or leave and admit defeat. One Heaven. One Hell. Not that I believe in either of those things but it's funny in times of severity how their notions come into play. My body had gone numb as if I were some quadriplegic that couldn't even mouth their joystick. I'm certain my expression was one of shock, eyes bulging like those blow-up dolls adults use to pleasure themselves in times of loneliness or when they're just too lazy to go through the rituals that get them in bed together; huffing fraught, masturbatory breaths into the vinyl receptacle as if their very existence depended on it, then having had their way, rid themselves of the evil whore by unplugging her and rolling her up into a little vinyl ball to hide in the back of their closet along with their stale despairing breaths.

A bump, a splash of booze laced soda cascading down my back and I was suddenly mobile and fighting through the crowd. Not far from the door I found myself prisoner in a perfume/cologne reeked gridlock. I became winded and fought for air. Through a rash of off-the-shelf dye-jobs and hair-plugged heads, penetrating the panicked buzzing in my ears came bits of adult banter:

'I can't drink beer, it gives me yeast infections.'

'The doctor said I could go to an herbalist, but that could take months if it worked at all. Better he burn them off.'

'Jessica Lange, is she not the most ultimate GILF?' (Grandmother I'd Like to Fuck.)

The room and its occupants tightened around me in a shrink-wrap of flesh. I became woozy; my head fell back and my eyes spun about the ceiling. On the verge of passing out and tasting *Eve-Ills* faux wood floor, I imagined *myself* an egg yolk being separated from its white and sucked up into a plastic water bottle then re-gestated into what I didn't know, but anywhere other than where I was. Someone bumped into me, and stumbling back I saw it, just feet away, standing before me like a holy grail, the exit door. I plowed through the throng and just as I reached out for that fake brass handle, just as I felt that taste of deliverance, there was Guy-Dick blocking my way, drink in hand. 'Down this and we'll get ta work.'

I have no idea how long I stood there. 'Come on kid there's no roofies in it, just a good shot-a-tequila. Ya look like ya need it.' I had no idea Guy-Dick was so chivalrous. I grabbed the glass and downed half of it. An abrupt burp and the tequila worked its way up and wrapped me in warmth.

I'm not much of a drinker, then even less so. Sure I'd had my standard youth experience, raided my parents' booze cabinet and went on an evening bender with typical teen consequences. Partnered in my adventure were my sister (before, and maybe what drove her into sainthood) her friend Dawn, and an un-cracked bottle of tequila; a forty-ouncer, or 'forty-pounder' as some of the assholes in school liked to call it. Like most tequila stories mine started out with the best of intentions: 'We'll just drink half, and save the rest for another time.'

Realizing we'd edged past our pencil line by maybe half an ounce the idea of saving the other 19 and 1/2 ounces seemed, well, just plain silly. Exposed in Dawn's parents' sunroom we drank it out of china teacups to fool any nosy neighbors. The china might have, but with the pristine windows being sprayed with projectile vomit, my projectile vomit, I venture to say our cover was blown. Once I'd emptied enough my sister heaved me into a cab in an effort to get us home before our parents.

The ride was harrowing, my sister half screaming directions and urging more and more speed, me behind the poor cab driver wailing for a higher power to stop the tsunami in my stomach. Ignored by that higher power I began panicking down the window. It was one of those windows that only go down halfway so I had to cock my head sideways to get it outside. As I projected into the winds the panicked driver began to pull over. My sister cried out to keep going, our parents' arrival being imminent!

At a red light only blocks from home a car pulled up beside us. Mouths agape the couple inside frantically gestured to their windshield, which was covered with my leavings, and under the fierce determination of their wiper-blades being smeared from stem to stern. Even in my rather fatigued state I knew what was coming next, them looking over to the culprit. Retreating my head inside I sank down behind the door revealing my sister to the outraged couple. Our parents.

I don't remember how I got my clothes off or getting to bed, but upon seeing my parents the next morning, both sitting grimly at the kitchen table, my father asked if during the previous night had I'd been drinking? I answered in true teen form. 'No.'

As the kitchen grew smaller and grimmer I voiced something to the effect of, 'Come to think of it, I did have a sip or two from my sister's friend's glass.' My mother asked about my puke-covered clothes. I proclaimed when I was helping her friend to the bathroom she'd gotten sick all over me.

Dad cleared his throat. 'So, that was not *your* vomit?'

True teen form: '...no.'

'No?' Dad asked.

'Yeah dad no, it was definitely her friend's.'

He sat back and shaking out his newspaper said, 'Well apparently *her friend* also shit in your pants.'

That was the last time I ever lied to my dad.

Anywho, Guy-Dick was about to buy me another tequila sunrise but with that bile-rising nostalgia hot in my throat I waved him off saying I was going home. Guy became animated wanting me to stay and take care of business, bully business. 'They need to pay. Just like the cops and judges and sleazy producers!' During his impromptu pep talk something became clear to me, across one side his face, a perfect handprint. Was it a curt goodbye from the twenty-something? Could I assume she wasn't, 'A 2 to 3 minute chick'?

Guy pressed for my plan, what did I want to happen to Al Kida, the issue suddenly more urgent in him than in me. I didn't know how to answer. I downed the last of my tequila, and as the drink continued to warm and comfort, instead of gripping its fake wood for support I began to relax against the bar. Rather than gasping for air I began to breathe. No longer feeling the center of attention I tried to refocus the situation. With my eyes acclimatizing to the sheen of overwrought make-up and nasal senses hardened to the grossly perfumed ambiance or perhaps just numb, something became clear to me. The atmosphere was one of joviality and their happiness, feigned or otherwise began to seduce me.

Guy-Dick was on to another twenty-something, and tried charming her with a joke. 'Have you heard about the new gay bar downtown? It's called *Leave it, it's Beaver!*' The twenty-something gaily responded, 'Oh it must be an old bar then, cause everybody shaves their beavers now.' Oh yes, the extinction of the beaver. I looked around trying to decide to whom to drop my bomb.

The bartender seemed a good choice, but I was leery of him getting a good look at my young face and questioning the legal status of my being there. To my left a man was laying another oldie but goldie on a sheen cadaver. 'What was the smartest thing to ever come out of Marilyn's mouth?'

'What?'

'JFK's cock!'

Yep...

Seeing my glass empty the bartender, a man with the thickest head of silver hair I'd ever seen (the Silver Beaver?) asked if I wanted another. Needing to blend I took him up on his offer but once in front of me I found it impossible to take a drink. Silver-Beav hung around and seemed to be waiting for a review of his work. Planting down on the straw I forced a small sip, nodded approval then abruptly coughed half of it up. He was quick with the napkins and I mentioned something of it going down the wrong pipe.

'Yeah... My wife's such a slob,' Silver Beav piped in, 'Every time I go to take a piss, the sink's full of dishes!' It seemed witticisms had become the evening's theme. As we chatted I laid the groundwork for my bomb. 'I'm looking for my father, he's been gone for days and my mother and siblings and I have run out of food and money.'

This sparked interest not just from Silver Beav, but from some men in the crowd and the jovialness that had creased their faces seemed to fade. Sensing an opening I leapt in, revealing Al Kida by his real name. I waited. And waited some more. No one had ever heard the name. WTF, I'd followed him there five times, he was a regular! I looked to Guy-Dick for help only to see him heading down the washroom corridor hand in hand with the beaverless twenty-something.

I repeated Al's real name slowly. Nothing. In the growing crowd of onlookers, I felt myself growing pale. I looked past Silver Beav to a faded newspaper clipping taped to the bar mirror. It was from the classifieds and the highlighted section read as such:

Utterly pathetic man seeks totally useless woman for entirely meaningless relationship.

Well didn't that just put everything into perspective? From inside my purse I yanked out a photo of Al Kida.

I'll describe the photo, one I'd stolen from his office. First off, Al Kida's office walls, his desk, his mantles were infected with portraits of himself. There were token few of his family, he, his wife and three young kids, all badly staged 'Say cheese' affairs you might find in some Wal-Mart frame. The countless others were of him glad-handing importants, you know, people more significant than him, future business targets he would no doubt take down by crushing in their business skulls. And then there was the solo gallery, Al Kida postured in a series of overtly imperative positions; addressing some great unseen audience; motioning to something in the sky; standing stalwart, hands in the air as if receiving some prodigious applause. The only one missing was a Darwinian pose of him holding a human skull, staring down into the shattered hole he'd created. Most of these seemed to have been taken in his home because the walls behind were festering with, guess what, more pictures of Al Kida.

I showed the photo to Silver Beav. But before he could fix on it a man took the picture from my not so giving hand (I knew I'd better get it back to Kida's office) and looked into it hard. I thought I saw a flash of recognition, but he was only registering a need for glasses which he began digging for in his suit. 'Oh my

God, it's Miguel!' said a woman snooping over the man's shoulder.

Miguel? Miguel was not his real name! Seemed Al Kida was haunting the establishment under a pseudonym, befitting behavior of a douchebag. I watched the woman reach from behind the guy, take the picture and flash it to the group she was standing with. I rushed to retrieve it but after making some indiscernible fuss over the photo the clutch of women passed it on. Helpless, I watched it make its way down the bar, clutched and re-clutched by one set of sweaty hands after another, Al's face becoming more and more disfigured by a thickening film of prints.

Silver Beav had moved down the bar and was getting a good look at the photo. He turned back to me and yelled above the din. 'What's the matter with him

'He's a home-wrecker!'

'You say he's gone?'

'I told you. He left us!'

'Kid, that's truly sad.' Silver Beav moved further away in the direction of the surfing picture. He said something to the new group of onlookers and a heated conversation broke out amongst them. I forged towards them and as I got closer I began to read their faces...the women, and I'll give them that the bar was rather warm, looked like wax figures that had been thrown into a tanning bed. I began picking up bits of their conversation:

'How did it happen?'

'I heard the house got wrecked on him.'

'What, a gas explosion?'

'Yeah, gone instantly.'

'Was he alone?'

'Was Miguel ever alone?'

'His daughter's here to take up a collection.'

In complete unison the faces looked up from the photo and right at me. I could see clearer, the women's goopy make-up was not running from heat, but from streams of tears.

'...Miguel's... left us...' blathered one of the goop dolls.

'You poor creature!' Another said to me.

'When's the funeral?'

Now there's broken telephone. 'No, he's not dead,' I exclaimed. 'He's a cheater!'

'Young lady, no one can cheat death.'

The Beav added, 'I'm...well, all of us here are sorry for your loss.'

I was besieged by a battering of condolences coming at me from all angles like I was a target in some video game. A tipsy teary man tried to console me with a hug but I sidestepped him right into a waitress with a tray of drinks. And like those lousy Hollywood movies where everything goes into slow motion, the colored liquids fountained up in the air, their colors melding into a virtual rainbow before tumbling back down, mostly over the waitress. On the verge of her about to explode on me one of the melting wax figures spoke up about my dad Miguel, and him having died from a terrorist's explosion. Upon hearing this the waitress who had somehow kept hold of the tray, let it slip from her grasp. More slo-mo as it landed on the floor careening like a giant coin until coming to a stop.

Things fell silent. Feeling cemented to the floor I looked around. The waitress broke into tears stirring the wax people into another eulogy of condolences.

'H-e w-as su-ch a be-auti-ful lov-er,' the waitress stuttered.

'I kn-ow, I kn-ow,' stuttered most every other woman in the assembly.

I looked around; except for a small cluster of free-range adults grazing on each other by doors it seemed the entire bar was in some state of grief. Then a man with a badly pockmarked face (it looked like a mob of vengeful stiletto sporting hookers had stampeded him) raised his glass. 'Let's have a moment of silence for our dear lost brethren, Miguel. A prince among swingers!'

Swingers? Really? I was alone in a fucking swinger's bar? Pockmark must have meant it for his stiletto-ridden face showed no trace of irony. The waxy philandering douchebags were turning Al Kida into a martyr!

I began edging back towards the doors. *Sh-tic! Sh-tic! Sh-tic! Sh-tic! Sh-tic!* Nearing the free-rangers I turned back towards the *Sh-tic* sounds and instantly my eyes were drawn upwards. The flames danced on the ceiling tiles like little stars. While tears coursed down faces or pooled in pockmarks, the crowd held blazing lighters in the air.

As if things weren't bizarre enough Pockmark broke into song: 'Danny Boy,' but shrewdly replaced 'Danny Boy' with 'Miguel Man.' Avoiding any eye contact I rushed through the choir and nearing entrance upended a hat that launched loose change and paper money into the air. I barreled out through the doors to the chorus of:

'Miguel man, your pipe's no longer piping...'

Despite wanting to run my legs refused to move with that kind of onus. Bound by shame they would only let me walk. I'd suffered my first defeat, more accurately Bullies Inc. had suffered its first defeat. There were no footsteps other than my own on that lonely walk home. I crawled under the sheets with a heavy heart. And for the first time in my life I cried myself to sleep.

40

At work, I was thrown onto several articles, like the semi-retired fireman who in his off hours raised an endangered species of insect, the Brychius Hungerfordi, a crawling water beetle. I mention this only as it being by far the most captivating. It seemed certain peers had a want for me to fail, and with material like that how could I fail their want? I asked for my two-week holiday and I got it, along with an offer of two more unpaid weeks. I refused the extra weeks; I wasn't about to walk through a door that would only close behind me. I would make the bully story a strong one, not so much to keep me there, but get me onto a better publication.

I still hadn't been able to talk to Courtney. That day at that restaurant I'd been distracted by the fainting girl and lost sight of Courtney. She'd been exchanging something with the waitress from the restaurant. At the time I guessed drugs, logical yet wrong. But who would have predicted what their exchange was really about? It would prove a journalist's fantasy. They say life is stranger than fiction, and they're right. Just look at the Kennedys.

I cancelled everything in my date book; dinner with my mother, personal appointments and all other engagements. Then I made a list of what I had so far:

-a flamboyant letter, warning retribution of a bully

-said bully arrested, not for bullying, but for child pornography??

-porn star arrested for planting the child porn onto said bully's computer

-said bully's victim exchanging money in a suspected drug deal

-and somehow orchestrating it all, most likely the letter writer, a mysterious Svengali-type teen

Looking it over I cursed myself for not having grabbed those other two weeks. What started out as a possible high school prank had turned into what could very well be a front-page headline. I was not about to let go of it, no matter how long it took.

In that spirit, I drafted my letter of resignation.

41

Though I walk through the Valley of the shadow of Dearth

FAILURE IS NOT AN OPTION! That's what they say. *They* being the ones who apparently never fail. I'd have loved to count myself amongst them, the forever victorious, but I could only count myself amongst the, not an option, failures. The defeat I'd suffered at Eve Ill's was cataclysmic, and rather than think back and try to sort through it, I deviated my time and energy onto others' problems, strangers' problems.

Summer was thriving in glorious technicolor bloom. Birds and insects sang its praises, night crickets chirped its splendor, and our backyard owl, the one I'd listened to for as long as I could remember but had never seen, hooted thumbs up. And there was me, unwilling to venture so much as a toe into all that gloriousness. I spent days and nights hiding myself in the dark of the rec room cloistered on the couch watching television. I became obsessed with daytime soap-stars lives, not just their character's lives but their real lives. WTF!

I considered drinking, but a sip of that thought raised a bile of opposition. I considered smoking pot; I'd tried it a few times. My first indulgence I didn't feel a thing save for sore lungs from coughing. The second time I got sooooooooo stoned I missed going home for dinner and by the time I did get there, dad banished me to dish duty.

It's not as if we didn't have a dishwasher, we had the latest and greatest. But one of dad's punishments was making us kids do the dishes by hand with the fucking dishwasher right beside the sink! Staring down into that soapy, foam-obscured water my stoned mind began to wonder... What was in there? Dishes sure, but...? I'd read of occurrences where rats, even snakes shot up through people's drains. And then I remembered, my dad is notoriously anti-drug.

Submerging my yellow gloves, I could feel the heat of the water but my hands remained cold. I began to hear the bubbles. They were talking to me. Crying out, one infinitesimal pop followed by another, each a tragic death wail! I grew teary and all the world's sadnesses – A sudden rustle of paper from the living room! Dad could speak with the newspaper, and over the years I'd learned its language. A quick rustle, Defcon 5, the lowest level could mean one of two things: *Turn down the television volume, or turn down your own volume.*

A louder, harsher rustle, let's say Defcon 3, could mean one or all three things: *Don't ask. Not now. Go to your room.*

Another rustle pierced the kitchen, this one harsher than the first. Defcon 2 or possibly Defcon 1, the harshest. I played it back in my head. I weighed it. I measured it. Then I – The gesture was repeated and I decided Defcon 2: *Get on with those damn dishes!*

Despite this logic I remained frozen, transfixed by those popping death cries. And from somewhere in the pity of my mind returned the sink invaders. I was stoned. So S-T-O-N-E-D!!! I broke out in a cold sweat. It seemed cold. But it could have been from the hot water I could no longer differentiate between hot and cold. Another Defcon (uncertain of its level) helped set in motion my sentence, and my right hand reached for a glass. In my home it was insisted glasses be done first while the water was cleanest, then silverware, then plates, then cookery such as pans and pots. Just as I reached for that first glass a small gasp of bubbles broke the surface. I yelped. And from the living room a rustle – Most definitely Defcon 1: *Don't make me have to get up and come in there!*

My hands dove back into the water and I was stacking glasses with a haste I'd never thought possible. 'I hope you're rinsing them out. Soap and Scotch do not mix!' Backpedaling I rinsed the glasses and in some cases scrubbed them.

By the time I hit silverware my soap bubbles had been silenced; the water a murky graveyard. Tears began rolling down my cheeks. Stacking some plates I began to panic. A massive wave of paranoia leveled me. What the fuck would I do once I'd finished the dishes? On the way to my room I'd have to pass dad and he'd stop me to say goodnight. He'd see I was stoned – Me getting shipped off to rehab to collect those little plastic medallions that I'd show my family on visitor's day? I heard no approach. 'So you're on that pot?'

I whirled around. Dad towered over me. How'd he know? How do parents always know? He stood just inches away, waiting for an answer. I couldn't lie, couldn't risk another tequila mortification that would haunt me the rest of my days. I needed to get ahead of it: *Dad, yes, it is me who has shit my pants*, so to speak. Once out there I'd fall on his court and beg for leniency! 'Dad, yes –'

He reached past me and lifted something from the sink. What he lifted was what I'd been in the middle of scouring, a pot. 'I told your mother these copper pots are hell to wash, but it looks like you're doing a pretty good job.' A kiss on the forehead and he was gone. Just like that. I scrubbed, dried then escaped to my bedroom and under the covers. It was 9:17 on a Saturday night. It was the last time I ever smoked pot.

Anywho, in the dark of the rec room my depression grew. As did my concern to whether Chad was truly the father of Dakota's second born Kennington, or had he in fact, as he had so often and wholeheartedly claimed, had a vasectomy upon divorce from his first wife Tatum, this after their son Thorold had grown into a teen serial arsonist?

I was setting a groove in the couch, one of creased apathy. TV besieged me with a new and surprisingly fresh set of adverts. A flock of commercials for diapers, but these little ditties were not for the smiling, laughing, cute-as-a-button babies. No these ingenious little thirty-second sound and picture bites were for adults. And like so many other commercials for adult sanitary products, the wearers of said merchandise, once garbed in them, seemed unable to be still. It used to be some sanitary-padded woman jogging or riding a bike or bouncing atop a very white horse, but the world of advertising had clearly progressed. In these new ads they danced!

Bumping and grinding as if reborn from soiling themselves. I wondered...

Now it's one thing to scoff at such television wisdoms, become a naysayer, spit on something without ever having experienced it. Was I one of those nay-spitters? Yes, I realized, I was. So laying there in my ever-deepening body groove, watching the shimmying ladies who seemed somehow ecstatic they'd just pissed or shit themselves, I thought. And I thought some more...

You see I'd hate for someone who, hearing about this memoir and all its bully reprisals, before giving it any kind of chance, denounced it out of hand. You know as if it was nothing more than say...*the Devil's work*, or the work of a *Psychopath*. Was I about to let myself fall into that closed-minded denouncement of a person? No-sir-re-Bob. That's another term of Gramps: '*No-sir-re-Bob!*' Bob not withstanding, watching those commercials to the point I could lip sync the narrator's joyful diatribe, I decided to open my mind, expand my view and cross over, as They say.

I needn't wait long. The little I'd been eating, mostly under-ripe fruits and a smattering of junk food proved a capricious combination. In that short spell of time I also waited for my favorite soap to make its appearance. Would Chad's sperm prove to be void in the sense of him truly having had a vasectomy and was now shooting blanks proving his now-wife Dakota's second pregnancy with Kennington was not his? And would Chad and his previous wife Tatum's arsonist son Thorold be going to go to prison, or a mental institution?

Inside me things were rapidly descending, while on television two actors from some TV show were gushing and marveling over how their android characters were so utterly human. Do these fucking people ever listen to themselves? Before I could answer that query all hell broke loose. Apt to do after a lifetime of the practice I started off the couch for the washroom. Pure force of will conquered the practice and I regained my slant on the couch and let nature take its course. Now at the time I was not wearing one of the boogying diapers, but I figured my briefs and sweat pants combined a reasonable facsimile. As fate would have it one of the frantic diaper commercials coincided with my movement and as I bore the fruit of my labor the dancing women ecstatically jived away. And then I began to wonder, were we supposed to think these euphoric women, at the same time they were wiggling and shimmying, were also urinating or defecating? Had any of the focus groups been asked this question?

I won't drag you through any more detail other than to say: 'EWWWWWW!' But along with that EWWWWWW came an epiphany. What I'd done to myself in that moment had become a monumental tonic, because only then, as I lay in my own filth, was I truly able to comprehend how depressed I'd become. Self-diagnoses sure, but who at that very moment was coming close enough to offer a second opinion?

I leapt off the couch straight for the washroom. I have to little jig, just to see if those commercials were all they were cracked up to be. They weren't.

Two showers. A bath. Then another shower before I felt ready to reclaim life. I turned all attention to Bullies

Inc. Thinking back on the week I felt more than remiss for my lack of leadership; if I'd been under the scrutiny of a board of directors they surely would've fired my recently soiled ass. But I was both board and CEO, so I offered myself another chance and gladly took it.

I would not focus on Al Kida. The purely adult world was just too overwhelming. I would turn all attention back to Bo Leemic. She would pay and this realignment would be by my own hand!

42

Precious days ticked by without anyone returning my calls. Courtney and her mother were silent. I left a handful of messages on Guy-Dick's phone, and then learned his number was taken out of service. And the waitress from the restaurant who had exchanged something with Courtney, my last real clue to the puzzle, was absent from work.

I grew despondent. I wanted, needed the story, the story all the others in the office had passed on. You know the term, 'One man's trash is another man's treasure'? The print media is very much like that. One reporter tosses aside what looks like story trash; another takes that trash, digs into it, and presto, leading item, front-page gold. But gold was not presenting itself. The night of the sixth day I could not sleep. I wrestled with

what I'd accumulated so far, and how I might
weave it into something substantial; perhaps
make a mystery out of the Svengali girl. But in the
middle of my weaving I was slapped with a
realization—Are you insane? On the issue of the
Svengali girl you're taking the word of a porn
star! Wake the #*^% up. I wished I could have
woken up, because that would have meant I'd
actually been asleep. When I did finally doze off it
was to the shrill of morning birds.

On the afternoon of the seventh day I received
a call from Courtney's mother who wanted to talk.
I raced through a shower, and was in the car
before I realized I'd never asked about Courtney.
Would she be there? I needed nothing more from
the mother, just Courtney.

Her mother ushered me into her home with a
hush reserved for Midnight Mass. My eyes swept
the hallway and living room for Courtney, but
found no trace of her. On the drive over I'd made a
plan to not sit where I had before, placed between
mother and daughter. People are creatures of
habit and I hoped changing our earlier seating
arrangement might throw them a little. The more
off balance, the more my questions might
penetrate their armor. But without Courtney the
only thing off balance was my plan. Still, I
changed from my previous seat and sat exactly
where Courtney had, cramped on the tip of a long
couch.

Outside the day was breezy and alive with life.
Inside the mood was more like a wake. As before

most of the curtains were drawn, but this time the mother kept getting up and tucking them tighter, as if she were under some kind of surveillance. We skipped around topics like the weather, the recent property-tax hike, climate change, and then she offered me some coffee which I was grateful for, if only for the break.

With mother in the kitchen I strolled around the living room hoping the creaking floorboards might draw Courtney. Hearing nothing in the house except the slow the drip of the coffeemaker I began to wonder if Courtney was even there.

The mother returned to the living room with a tray of coffee and condiments, but she looked different. The fresh redness in her eyes made me think she'd been crying. As we dashed our drinks with cream and sugar she began to speak of bullies. But no longer did she speak of them as if they were scourges of the earth; rather she wanted to understand them.

Why they did what they did. Were they broken people? Could they be helped?

I was taken aback. Had the woman switched from categorical bully condemner to someone bearing empathy? I needed to keep her talking so I might find a clue to her behavioral shift, but sitting in the darkness of the window the woman seemed to withdraw. Hoping she'd open to me, I opened to her about my own bully behavior. She sparked to this, but as I explained it was just me trying to fit in, me trying to became part of a nasty high school clique, she shut down altogether. I cajoled. I pried. My coffee, good as it was, went cold, but I could gather nothing as to what had happened. But clearly something had.

Finally a pleading came into her eyes, and I could see she wanted to tell me something. I asked after Courtney, would she be joining us? The mother looked to the floor and after a time, shrugged. A breeze blew back one of the curtains and it slashed across her face. She made no effort to move it away. I felt a sudden need to get out of there.

A heart-jarring BANG as the front door opened and crashed off the doorstop. Courtney's mother shot up and looked towards the hallway. The floorboards creaked approach and into the living room walked her daughter. Courtney looked past her mother as if she wasn't there, to me, and best as I could tell, grinned. I could see a change in her. The clothes, the hair and make-up were the same, but rather than the fearful expression that previously gripped her face, it seemed fixed in some kind of darkness. Her mother asked her to sit. Courtney said she was only home to change her clothes and going right back out. It was not so much a statement, but a command.

The dynamic between mother and daughter had entirely reversed. Another floor creak and this one sent the mother's look to the floor. From the hallway she strolled into the living room, up to Courtney, and standing beside her said hello to the mother. It was the girl from the restaurant, the skinny waitress who had shared some kind of exchange with Courtney. Together they stomped upstairs to Courtney's bedroom, shut the door behind them, and once again the living room lapsed into silence.

I watched the oils from my coffee cream congeal into a fractured smile. The mother asked if I wanted more. She was suddenly standing in front of me, her coffee suffering the same fate as mine. I thanked her no, and asked how Courtney was doing. 'She's not scared anymore, if that's what you're after.' I tried to assure her that was not what I was after, I simply wanted to follow up and learn how her daughter was doing. The mother's hand began to tremble. The china cup rattled off its plate as if the entire house were shaking. Coffee sluiced over the sides and her white knuckled fingers looked about to break through the plate. I reached out to steady her hands but a sudden severe trampling drew my attention to the stairs.

Reaching the bottom, Courtney stopped long enough to stamp into some runners. I rose from my chair and asked how she was coping with things? 'Ya mean with the bullying?' I felt her peering into me. 'Yes, how are you doing with the bullying?' Her response continues to send chills through me. There's the term: Time heals all wounds. John Lennon put a twist on it: 'Time wounds all heels.' Courtney put her own twist on it: 'Time wounds all whores!'

The waitress friend giggled. Courtney did not share her reaction; rather she stared straight at me, said something to her mother about not being home for dinner, and slammed out. I looked back to her mother, still standing in front of me, a dozen questions perched on my tongue, but something in her despairing expression told me to keep them there.

I found myself walking to the door unaccompanied, and without turning back said goodbye and left. In my goodbye I was unable to hide a tone of apology, though I wasn't sure for what. Courtney no longer seemed afraid, good thing. She was with a friend and not isolating herself, often a reaction to having been bullied, another good thing. So what was I apologizing for? She had definitely been through something, but what?

I felt a washout. Why hadn't I pressed it? I should have gone after the mother and tried to shake the story from her, to learn about the change in Courtney. Driving home my mind replayed the visit. I'd noticed when Courtney said, 'Time wounds all whores'—the waitress had mouthed along with her. There was something there, some conspiracy between the girls. Sure, they were teens that can fire up conspiracies faster than a flipped burger, but for me, coupled with the mother's strange behavior, the moment really spooked me. But what exactly was the moment? What were those girls up to?

Knowing she would recognize me, I could no longer follow Courtney. The same went for the waitress. Again I kicked myself for not having pressed them while I had the chance. Fear boiled over. I wasn't cut out for the world of journalism and all its requisite prying. Once inside my apartment I called my travel agent to see if he could find me a reasonably priced escape.

I lay in the tub long after the water turned cold, long after my body turned to something resembling a long white raisin, my only movement was to answer my cell. 'Please Jerry, I don't care, Barbados, Bahamas, a banana Republic in the middle of a communist coop, just tell me you can get me out tonight.'

'I've got something I think you want, baby.'

A chill ran through me. It definitely was not Jerry my travel agent. 'Who is thi –' I didn't finish my question...it was Guy-Dick. Naked in the tub a wave of vulnerability crept over me. He could have been calling from Russia, the Himalayas, the moon, I just couldn't handle the idea of being naked on the other end of Guy-Dick. 'Hello, I didn't think I'd hear from you again.' Grabbing the towel rack I carefully drew myself up from the water, hoping not to make any noise.

'In the tub, huh? Bubbles? Oils? Rubber duckies?'

'So how've you been Guy?' Stepping out I knocked the plug with my toe, so the remainder of our conversation played to the sound of draining water.

'I've been real gooooood.'

I couldn't tell if he was trying to sound good-humored, or did he just have a talent for making everything he said sound invasive? I was dripping and cold. 'So, you have something I might want?'

'Oh not might. Baby, you want it!'

'And how's that Guy?'

'I scratch your back. You scratch mine.'

'Yea, no back scratching Guy, literally or metaphorically.'

'What's...met...a –'

'Don't worry about it. You have information for me and for it you want something in return. Am I right? You have something you want to trade for something else?'

'Yeaaa. Some...thing...like...that.'

Invasiveness bled into creepiness. 'Okay, so do you want to meet or something?'

'Meet?'

'Yes, meet.'

'Meet where?'

It was like talking to a child. 'How bout the same place as last time?'

'Okay sure...wai...what place was tha—oh ya mean where I puked an' shit?'

I was surprised he even remembered. 'Good call, Guy.' I suggested a place, public of course, and busy at that time of the day. He then made me recite not only the address, but directions on how to get there, claiming he had no use of a computer due to his legal battle with the 'Asshole legal system!' This I did, repeating the directions over and over, practically syllable-by-syllable until I realized... the noises on the other end of the phone were not those of pen to paper.

As the last of my bathwater gurgled down the drain, with my ears fixed on his heavy breaths, the call display lit up with my travel agent. Diving for the call I told Guy to meet me in an hour. Notwithstanding I'd just had an hour-long bath, I felt very much in need of another.

43

That's Why He Walked!

So the story goes: a couple holidaying in the Middle East find themselves on the shore of the Dead Sea. There they approach a tour guide who's offering passage across the sea in a small passenger boat. The husband asks how much, and the guide answers one hundred dollars per person. The husband turns to his wife and says, 'A hundred dollars each? No wonder Jesus walked!'

I felt like that tour guide, offering a most legitimate service only to find myself the butt of a joke. I also felt like the husband being hustled for $; i.e. Van Detta, Goon 86, and Guy-Dick insisting payment for what was in essence a hallowed event, one which they should've been happy to donate their services. Fuck'em, I thought, just me from now on. Now I'm quite small in stature and have never taken boxing or martial arts or killing with a sword classes or anything. My entire life I've had only two physical fights, and lost both.

I returned to my sister's place of business on her day off, ready to reconnect with Bo Leemic, hoping to find inspiration when looking into her nasty face. The place was hopping. A heat wave had attacked the city and the streets were mostly barren, malls, movie theatres, restaurants packed with people avoiding being broiled. There'd been so many folks, not just kids, but adults cracking eggs on the sidewalks a town ordinance was decreed and fines of $48.75 were issued to any and all violators. But how can anyone put a price on science?

I wasn't able to get a seat in Bo's section but made a point of waving to her. Her greeting was less than enthusiastic, her expression stony, unreadable and truth be told, unnerving. I left the crowded eatery but rather than buy some eggs and risk a $48.75 fine (if one hatched an entire dozen on an unsuspecting sidewalk would the fine be prorated to $585?), I hung out in the mall and waited for Bo to finish her shift. My plan was to *'bump into her'* as she left work for the day, not ingenious but not unreasonable. I browsed stores and picked up the latest CDs by two girl punks bands, The Glory Wholes and The Cunning Stunts, and one by this punk boy-band, Armed and Hammered. I still prefer CDs to invisible MP3s. Life's already too intangible.

Biding time I glanced through my CD liner notes while line-ups to the local hero-movieplex formed like mindless human snakes only to be ingested by its array of strobing lights, bombastic previews, and its promise of reprieve from their tepid lives.

Time passed, one lineup ingested after another, and I began worrying Bo might be doing a double shift. That would mean me hanging around then 'bumping' into her after all the stores had closed which would make me look like a stalker or worse, a mall-rat. Her stony expression loomed.

She finally exited and started away under a head of steam. Unready for her speed I was too late to 'bump into her' and found myself trailing her. She veered through the mall-people like some torpedo, but a real one, not the Murder Inc. ones. Though the sun had begun to set the temperature outside was stifling. Having swallowed the sunrays the concrete and asphalt seemed to be retching them back like steamed bile. Bo didn't seem to mind it, or maybe she was just oblivious for her speed through the endless parking lot only increased and I found myself running to keep up. I had no idea where she was going but she was clearly on a mission to get there.

I was relieved when she landed at a bus stop because not only was I out of breath, from every pore in my body I was dripping sweat. Using the collar and sleeves of my T shirt I mopped up as best I could, then sauntered to the stop, pretending to read the back of one of my CDs. With love ballads like, *'I'm Heinous for Your Anus!'* it was hard to put it down.

'You following me?'

I looked up to find Bo cross-armed, waiting for an answer. I forced a smile. 'No I was just waiting for the bus. Not following you at all. I was just—

'I'm kidding.'

Getting to know someone is like going into a dark house and exploring it room by room, only it's their mind you're exploring. I didn't want Bo's entire tour; I wanted straight into the last room people take you, the basement. Looking into her eyes I could see her mood had shifted from the restaurant, not so...heinous.

'You live at this fucking mall or something?'

I couldn't tell if she was joking or prying. 'No, just wanted to get some music.'

Without being invited she took the CD bag and ripped through its contents. 'I have this one, but just like the MP3s. CDs are sooooo yesterday after dinner.' She went on, 'I love this tune, 'Don't Be Coy with My Toy, Go Punk On My Junk!' We had found communion! Eventually some of my own thoughts and words edged into the conversation that carried from music to movies; sadly Bo was into lousy Hollywood hero movies, but that made it easy to play along because, like most people into that trendy dreck, she assumed everyone had seen the movie in question, so all I had to do was nod affirmation every once in awhile.

Although her bus travelled opposite to mine I accompanied her and we continued our conversation moving from entertainment to clothes, hair, boys. She even went as far as describing some bullies in her school. Girl bullies she defined as I might. 'The scourge of the earth!'

I bit down on my tongue, hard, then asked if she'd ever been bullied? Bo went silent and turned to the window. Her reflection revealed tears, and I knew I'd really put my foot in it. I searched for something that might ease things; something to bring her back but my lack of social skills left me wordless. At the next stop she finally turned back to me. I tried not to look shocked. Her tears were not ones of pain. No, Bo Leemic was furious. She started to speak but her voice was so low and gravelly I couldn't make out what she said and was too afraid to ask her to repeat herself. She leaned close and whispered, 'That fucking bitch is gonna pay. And soon. She's fucking toast!'

And with that she asked to borrow two of my CDs, took the bag from my stunned hands, slipped out the discs, said to drop by the restaurant anytime tomorrow as she'd be working a double, then ringing the dong stepped out the door without another word.

Two stops later I got off, crossed the street and waited for the bus home. So in shock I failed to notice the heat, which I believe was frying my brain because not until later, after cooling down in the air-conditioned rec room did it become clear to me. The 'She' Bo was talking about was my sister! And when Bo said, 'And soon' did that mean next week? Tomorrow? Would I have to realign her straight away? Physically I stood no chance against her, if only due to her artificial scalpel-like nails.

That night I didn't sleep at all. My mind spun against how Bo was going to '*Make my sister pay!*' And how exactly I would make Bo pay. Then some time around dawn's crack I got up and, rushing to the washroom, violently threw up. And while the morning birds sang in a brand new day, hanging over the toilet I watched the little contents of my stomach form into something resembling a smiley face.

44

Why had I picked a vegetarian restaurant with no air conditioning? Usually crowded with aware and un-inebriated people, the place was not only void of patrons, patrons I might count on to be witness in case something happened, but in the extremely hot weather it had become a sweatbox. My question in choosing a veggie restaurant is mostly rhetorical; I knew they did not serve alcohol. I could not bear to see Guy-Dick get sloppy drunk and throw up again. Near the bottom of a second cup of green tea he sauntered in in a one-piece boiler suit. Before reaching my table he stopped and sniffed the air. 'What the hell's that?'

Vegetarian restaurants have their own fragrance, but it wasn't so much what Guy-Dick smelled, it was what he didn't smell, the absence of grilled animal flesh and fat drippings. Guy-Dick worked past his revulsion, and took a seat in a creaky wooden chair across from me. I mention the creaky part because for the rest of our meeting he leaned forward and back, playing the chair like a kid who's just gotten his first drum set. 'It's boiling in here. Where's the AC? Are these guys livin' in the @%#* stone-age?'

The waitress approached. Sizing her up, Guy-Dick said somewhere in the kitchen there must be booze, and why didn't she just go back there and sneak him some out. Then raising two fingers to his temple Guy declared a 'Scout's honor' promise not to tell her boss. Informing him she was not only the boss, but also owner of the establishment, the woman managed to get him off the subject of liquor, and Guy asked for a double espresso. She thusly informed him, due to technological advances that have caused coffee growing to have a nasty effect on the environment they no longer served coffee, and in any case there were no benefits in the consumption of coffee, and that its by-product, caffeine, not only alters our body's functioning, but is highly addictive. Guy-Dick was at a loss. I stepped in and ordered him some frozen yogurt, the closest thing I could think to a bowl of ice cream.

This next part, and I've really grappled on whether or not to include it, has little to do with the story. It's what we call character-color, a bit of background on the person of interest. Between grinning mouthfuls of frozen yogurt Guy-Dick went into his new 'genius' idea of how to revive his slumping porn career. I'll abbreviate as much as possible.

He spoke in great detail of being uncircumcised, a point of pride for Guy-Dick, and how in the porn business 'An uncut man' was a rarity. But things being as they were, he'd decided to 'Get cut.' Sure yea, sounds great Guy –

But just as I tried to move things onto his information, he rambled on, saying that in order to stand out from the other men of porn, he was going to get what he called a 'Fancy cut.' Morbid curiosity having got the better of me, I asked what that meant. Guy clamored on, vowing all they'd done for centuries is the same, boring, even cut. He then faked a yawn, I have to admit he had perfect teeth, and went into his plan. In unequivocal detail he described a parade of circumcised penis styles: a Slanted Bob, much like the haircut with one side of his foreskin hanging longer than the other; a Mohawk, short at the sides and long down the middle; a King's crown, long-short-long-short all the way around, then the Odango, where two buns are worn on each side. 'Like that chick's hair in Star Wars, only foreskin!' Guy ended his runway pageant with a final circumcision option, the Archie comic's character, Jughead Jones's, multi-pointed hat. I checked Guy's pupils. If they hadn't been normal, and he hadn't been so serious, I would have laughed out loud, or maybe cried.

Guy-Dick sat staring, fingers drumming the tabletop, waiting out my response. My mouth opened, but nothing came out. Do I pick one, and then get roped into debating its merits over the others? Do I suggest he get the old, boring, even cut? Do I suggest he check himself into a mental facility? I went with the Jughead. I've always disliked those comics.

My suggestion went unacknowledged and I found myself in a half-hour deliberation that felt more like a month. But there was no getting to whatever information he had without measuring the pros and cons of each circumcision style. I couldn't help think my mother might have been right about a career in journalism, my head felt very much mounted on a pike.

Guy ended up stuck between the King and Mohawk cuts. I told him I thought both good choices, and again pressed him for the reason of our meeting. After adjusting himself under the table he told me there was no way he'd give me that info without me first buying him a drink. I was too committed to the story to refuse. Guy-Dick said he was tired of this meatless, alcohol-less, sweat box, and insisted we go, 'Where there's pounds'a meat, gallons'a booze, and the only things sweaty are the 'flesh pies!'

45

Mourning in the Evening

We were having dinner at our neighbors', a once-a-month event that claims the un-checkered history of being entirely unremarkable. We've known them for years; know their kids Josh and Mandy though we've never really hung out, but our parents and their parents hung out; sharing junkets to the theatre, the opera, the ballet; sampling all the meats of our city's cultural stew.

Anywho, on this occasion the daughter Mandy was absent, called into her workplace to fill in for an 'unwell colleague' was the story given upon our arrival. During drinks dad cracked a joke about his colonoscopy exam. 'And ever since the damned doctor keeps sending me Valentine's Day cards!' Yeah dad, nice.

After the picture-perfect chicken cordon bleu – our neighbors love to put on a show – the mother's hand, while about to torch my desert, began trembling. Now I don't mean that fake Hollywood, *Hey look! I'm showing you how fucked up I am, so where's my fucking Academy Award* handshaking, I mean scary handshaking to the point of shuddering out the blowtorch she was using to caramelize my crème brûlée.

Despite the mishap she persisted, the torch's relit flame bounding between my pudding and my face.

Being the *ultra-polite suburbanites* we were, my dad, mom, big sister, little brother, the flame-thrower's husband and 10-year-old son, kept quiet, all eyes glued to the torch that now wavered from my crème brûlée to the flammable tablecloth dangling over my bare legs.

Slipping from her tremulous grip the blowtorch crashed off the hardwood sending our shoulders to our ears. The mother, bottom lip trembling, fled the dining room and ran down a hall slamming some unseen door behind her. Our gazes turned from the hallway to her husband. At length he lifted his face from his hands, got up, walked towards me, picked up the blowtorch and gently placed it on the table; too close to a flaming candle for my liking. He looked to us with graveness. An excruciation of seconds followed. Voice quietly catastrophic the father went into the reason for his wife's unstable blowtorch operating and her curt, unannounced exit from the table. Seemed their absentee daughter Mandy – Hang on, first I have to share this part. Their dating song, the husband and blowtorch wife, their hook-up song, the one they played for their wedding dance and pretty much every time we went over there, was that old Barry Manilow ditty called 'Mandy.' You know:

'Oh Mandy, you came and you gave without taking.
And I sent you away.
Oh Mandy, you kissed me and stopped me from shaking.
And I need you today!'

And yes, the tune was the inspiration in naming their daughter.

So the bump to the hitherto unremarkable evening was he and his family learned their dear daughter, sweet little Mandy, had become a stripper.

I looked down to my un-caramelized crème brûlée and tried to focus against laughing. And in my focus I began rearranging the song lyrics to better fit the situation:

Oh Mandy, you stripped and you twerked without faking.
And I gave you my pay.
Oh Mandy, you lapped me and started me shaking.
And I feel like prey!

Unable to help myself from inappropriate laughter, I squinted (as if that might seal it away) and looked back up. Dad, mom, sister, brother, stripper-dad and stripper-little-brother sat silent, mouths agape, staring at me with a fused, horrified expression. Seemed my whispering of the tune was not just in my head.

My sister, bless her heart and trembling lower lip – the damned things were mesmerizing – broke into tears, which seized attention from me and launched my mother from her chair. Throwing out a lineage of apology to stripper-father, stripper-son and absentee stripper-mother (her abandoned cries echoed down the hall) mom grabbed hold of my sister and little brother, who for the first time in our six years of attending these functions was finally engaged in the goings-on, and hustled them to the door. She called for me to follow, but with her hands full and dad busy consoling the father I slid into the living room and out of sight. The unremarkable evening was shaping into something quite remarkable.

Realizing any attention would draw dad into a conniption of banishing me home, I dared not move. Then, having caught the contagion of the trembling lower lip, stripper-brother Josh cried out he wanted things to go back to the way they were. 10 years old and already in the grips of nostalgia. Where does one go from there? He stumbled down the hall to what I can only assume was his mother. I watched dad console stripper-father, his awkward arm barely touching the man, as if any real contact would send him into a similar lamentations. *Mourning in the Evening.*

From the hall the lamenting rose in pitch and volume, stripper-mother and stripper-brother's yowls harmonizing with the baritone moans of stripper-father. Though somewhat transfixed by the improv concerto I realized if it continued unabated, the suddenly remarkable evening would dissolve through my fingers into a river of tears and snot and going home unrequited. I needed to turn things around. 'Dad, why don't we do an intervention?'

Dad looked to me unblinkingly. I couldn't tell if he was surprised I was still there, or by what I'd said. 'Really dad, why don't we just go get her and bring her back so they can talk it out?' I motioned to stripper-father who looked at me as if I was some haloed messiah. *Dude, ever watch TV, this one's a no-brainer!* Dad thought this was a sterling idea and leapt onto his white horse, in this case a blue Subaru station wagon, and dragging me by the arm for support or perhaps as a witness, told stripper-father we were going do the 'Right thing.'

In the car, as he shifted into reverse, dad stopped, as did my heart. Had his bubble of heroism burst? With the night having opened its heavens of possibility, was he about to send me home? Turned out dad didn't know where the strip club, Tight-Spaces was so he rushed back to the house to ask directions.

Tight-Spaces' parking lot spoke of its clientele; it looked more like a scrapyard than a place for licensed automobiles. Dad zipped into one of the last parking spaces, leapt out, barked an order, waited until I put up the windows and locked the doors then made his way through the slightly ironic wide double doors of Tight-Spaces. It was better than any fucking movie!

Keeping an eye on the entrance I rifled through dad's CD collection hoping for some Barry Manilow; the closest I came was the best of Peabo Bryson. Don't ask. Creating my own soundtrack to the evening I continued my rendition Mandy, but more spiritedly than I had at the dinner table:

Oh Mandy, I came, so you get off that pole now…

Headlights poured across the club illuminating sternly painted stripper silhouettes. I watched the seedy clientele enter with zip and exit with zap, but no dad or Mandy.

Oh Mandy, are you not working today?
Are you givin' it away?

The song was writing itself!

Somewhere in the middle of the final chorus I realized dad had been gone a long time. What was taking him? Had I facilitated dad getting into something beyond himself? Perhaps a dust up with the bouncers, those neck-less over-muscled bullies who'd feed his head to his butt? Or had the girls gotten to him, you know tackled and piled onto poor old dad like they do in football, creating a yeasty, chlamydia-infested compress?

Kicking open the car door like one of those lousy Hollywood action-stars I stormed to the entrance. I was greeted by one of those neckless troglodytes with biceps as big as my hips who grinned and asked if I was, 'Lookin' for work?'

For a fleeting moment I considered hiring the bouncer for Bullies Inc. – the massive ape would only have to stare down on say, Bo Leemic, to frighten her into a public bowel-voiding which would annihilate her teen reputation, which would destroy her more than any physical or mental atrocity I could ever manage or imagine. But was the moment right for professional headhunting? I thought to ask him for his business card, but right then dad surfaced with a mascara-streaked Mandy, his jacket draped over her. Dad, forever the nobleman. I was ordered back to the car and made to sit in the backseat with Mandy, whose lower lip, like the rest of her family's, trembled hypnotically.

As we began pulling out of the parking lot, dad's headlights exposing the lurid front doors, out popped none other than Guy-Dick! He seemed perplexed, alarmed even, looking after Mandy like she'd stolen his heart, or maybe his wallet. And even more disturbing, following on his heels was the woman reporter!

We locked eyes and in our stare, I felt destiny coming straight at me.

46

She stared straight at me, the girl who'd passed out in the restaurant. Guy-Dick was pointing her out, cursing her for the stripper having quit halfway through his third lap-dance. I was more than relieved, watching a young girl perform simulated sex acts on a man's lap really wasn't my thing, but watching her perform to a Barry Manilow love ballad bordered on surreal.

Sitting in the back seat beside the stripper, the girl seemed unable to look away from me, or maybe I was unable to look away from her. Guy continued yelling, saying she was the one I wanted; the ringleader of the group called Bullies Inc. Ignited by the car's headlights the frantically waving Guy-Dick cut quite a picture, and was quickly ushered away by the bouncers. I memorized the car's plate number and hoped a friend at the DMV might be able to help me out.

47

Your Karma's running over my Dogma

If I were truly clever I'd have found a way to realign Bo and Al Kida at the same time. I sweated over how I might make that happen, but with cleverness eluding me I continued my excruciating act of making a friend of Bo Leemic.

Stalking the mall whenever my sister wasn't working —Okay, I hate malls and I hate mall people. And there's a term, Overcrowding. I can't say the mall was overcrowded, but some of its inhabitants most definitely were.

Clothes come with too many fucking labels, 60% this, 20% that, no iron, must iron, tumble dry, no dryer, hand wash, dry clean only. And I don't care to know if some child laborer using his or her initials or simply a number, Inspected by #187, really checked and gave my underwear the green light. I mean if there's a problem with my underwear can I call the company and get child laborer #187 on the phone? Clothing companies should devote their efforts to more important labels, labels referring to such topics as *overcrowding*. I mean elevators have them – Maximum capacity not to exceed 10 persons or 2500 pounds. Clothing should have similar warnings, and unquestionably these should include cheaper lines of sweat-wear and anything made of spandex. WARNING: Maximum capacity not to exceed 300 pounds. I'm sure science can stretch a baby-buggy tire around a truck rim, but how do you think that would look? Just because you can TORTURE YOUR FAT ASS into THAT SPANDEX doesn't make IT A GOOD fit!

Amidst the bloated parade of mall people Bo appeared, cutting her way through the lard-arsed like the proverbial knife through butter. Though I hadn't realized it at the time, her 'borrowing' my two CDs was a perfect excuse for coming back to see her. And it made me think, as CEO of Bullies Inc., these are the kinds of things I need to spot ahead of time. Bo went straight into the restaurant so I hung around contemplating more pressing and urgent clothing-tags until she finally took her break. I waved a surprised hello and followed her into the parking lot where she sucked down two cigarettes with such intensity I imagined smoke exhaling from her ass.

Bo's condemnation continued to stew in me, 'Believe me, she's fucking toast!' As she lit her second cigarette I toed into the waters of how she was going to toast my sister, without mentioning my sister outright. Bo smiled that sour smile one does when they have something you want, and they know you want it, and they know they don't have to give it to you. The one that makes you want to kick their teeth out so never again can they flash a smile, sour or otherwise, unless of course they get dentures, but then the fear becomes the teeth coming unglued and, 'Clack.'

Through heated exhales she told me she was contemplating telling me more about it, 'Maybe,' but we'd have to meet later and discuss it then, 'Maybe.' I was to meet her in the same woods Van Detta had realigned Joe-Bow. Seemed my bully dealings had come full circle.

That night, just like some cheap Hollywood movie, the moon was full, or close to it. Alone within the trees and shrubbery I eyed the maple that had taken the lightning hit, the 'Burning Bush,' its top half blackened and dead. I tried to replay that night and its almost biblical realigning, but like reaching for sanctuary in a dream, it eluded me.

The cracking of a twig and I spun in all directions. 'Bo?' I heard a breath. 'Bo?'

A breeze chilled through willow branches. 'B –' And then it hit me. What if Bo was getting me out here because I was the one she was going to 'toast'? She hadn't actually said it was my sister; I'd just assumed so. What if it was me? What if all that transpired was just a way of getting me alone in the fast darkening woods?

Though I'd worn my steel-toed combat boots I had no idea how to use them. Sure I could kick, but with what kind of accuracy? And if I missed or maybe just skinned her, what kind of wrath would I draw? Would Bo and all her bad Karma crush me and my Bullies Inc. Dogma?

A crashing through the woods sent my blood screaming. I panicked about, looking for something I might wield in trying to defend myself. The only thing of substance was a fallen blackened branch about ten feet long. Whatever was coming I was at their mercy.

The crashing grew louder and I could feel each unforgiving step through my boots. Was it more than one? I set my feet and stood tall or tried to, like those fish that blow themselves bigger to scare away their predators. Through the last bit of shrubbery some final stomping and into the clearing she stood, beer in one hand, cigarette in the other. Bo Leemic looked like some lousy Hollywood exposé of misguided youth. 'Hey, fergot the... yur... sor... what... ah... CDeees.... haha... sorry...' She chuckled at this; though I couldn't be sure what she was chuckling or sorry about. Was it the CDs, was she was sorry for not bringing them or sorry they were no good and laughable? Or was she sorry for her mangling of the English language? Teens make terrible drunks. I tried to sound cool, 'It's okay,' but I had no idea what my 'okay' really meant. She laughed and said they sucked then laughed again and said she was joking then laughed again and asked if I wanted a beer?

I didn't, but there was no saying no. Performing illegal acts, teens become mistrustful, and someone refusing participation raises fears you might be a rat, and then you find yourself alienated. I needed Bo. I took the offered beer, popped the top and took a slug. Ewwwwww – yet effective because before its lousy tang finished frothing down my throat Bo threw a friendly arm around me and told me there was someone I had to meet. I WAS IN!

She blathered on for a bit then suddenly claimed this person had a big bone to pick with me. Bo withdrew her arm and the smile faded from her face. A crushing of ground twigs. Someone else began breaking through the shrubbery. I gripped my beer can and mentally aimed it at whoever was making their way towards me. Bo turned to the sound and I had flashes of those lousy Hollywood movies where I would grab her from behind and hold a knife or box cutter or sword to her throat and threaten the oncoming intruder with Bo's death. But I had no knife or box cutter or sword and worse, I hadn't the chutzpah to do it anyway.

More thrashing and finally someone emerged from the shrubbery. I'm not sure this ever really happens, but I'm pretty sure my jaw dropped. Before me, ghosting under the glow of the moon stood Courtney. Now why would she have a big bone to pick with me? All I'd ever done was save her from Anna Rexic and her cyber bullying!

'So, it's you.'

That's all she said. Courtney I mean. How best to answer that? A simple 'Yes,' or something with attitude, 'No, I'm a clone. You're looking at a fucking clone!' They stood side by side like some lousy Hollywood teen death squad. I looked down to my steel-toed boots. They stared back at me like empty guns, but unlike some lousy Hollywood movie I couldn't throw the discharged weapons at the teen death squad. And why does anyone think that'll ever work? When's the last time you heard of a cop emptying his weapon then throwing it and knocking out the perp? 'Thank you all, but what you really need to thank is that extra week in the police academy: Throwing your empty weapon with criminal-crushing heft and accuracy, 101.'

And then it happened, just like some lousy Hollywood movie where someone breaks the moment of tension, Bo Leemic started laughing. But was her laughing, like in some lousy Hollywood movie, the kind where the bad guy finally pulls the trigger and it's really a water gun? Or was it some lousy Hollywood movie laughing the villain sports before slaughtering their victim? Before I could form another lousy Hollywood scenario Courtney joined in on the laughter. So I was the butt of some fucking joke? The two of them high-fived, then, gathering themselves, turned all attention on me.

'Ya got any money?'

I would have expected this from Bo Leemic, but it was coming from Courtney. 'Not much, maybe twenty bucks.'

'Ya know what happened to Courtney?' asked Bo.

I considered this might be trick question, some trap I might fall into. '...you mean the bullying?'

'Yea,' Courtney said. 'What else?'

I wondered if she understood the pitifulness in her asking, 'What else?' Was her life nothing but being bullied?

'Ya seem cool so we're gonna let ya in on it.'

Wow! Me asked to join others? 'Let me in on it?'

'We're gettin' 'er done.'

'Who?' I stressed to sound casual.

'Who else?'

'Right...' I stressed to sound casual.

'That fucking douche!'

With two certifiable douches facing me I stressed more, '...sure.'

'Ya wanna help?'

Quit being so fucking cryptic bitches! 'K.'

'Alright!'

Bo raised her hand and I obligingly high-fived it. I turned to Courtney but her hand was not raised in the friendly gesture. I forced a smile; one I hoped covered the fact I didn't have a fucking clue what they were talking about.

'If yer gonna help,' Courtney said, 'we need some cash.'

Even in teen world it always comes down to the almighty fucking $. They stood waiting for an answer. WTF were they talking about? '...how much?'

'Like...a grand.'

My expression must have given away my shock because both girls charged closer the way someone might in thinking the other person was about to pass out. 'You don't...it could be less. But like, isn't yur dad lawyer?'

Why do people assume all lawyers are rich? 'What's it for?'

They looked at each other in that conspiratorial way only teen girls can. 'Ya already said ya wanted to help.'

They had me there. 'K, but it's a lot of money and like...what's it for exactly?'

'We're gonna have her wacked.'

They had to be testing me. 'Who?'

'Anna Rexic,' Courtney stated. 'We know a gang dude who'll end her for a grand.'

In the resounding silence that followed, under the girl's waiting glare, something broke though my terror. The dispatching of bullies, Bullies Inc., was my fucking idea! Where did these douche bags get off plagiarizing me? Before I could respond they tag-teamed me with pitches, Bo Leemic going on about Anna Rexic driving Courtney to suicide, then Courtney prattling on about Bo also being a victim of Anna Rexic to which Ms. Leemic flashed me her scarred wrists.

'Why...don't you just get her beaten up?

'Cause the bitch deserves to die!'

'That's why!'

'Bitch gotta die!'

They even had a little rhymin' going on. Still, there was no fucking way. 'I can't get that much money.'

'We'll pay you back some of it. We just don't have any right now, ya know. Like we'll go halvsies with you.'

Halvsies? On murder we'll go *halvsies?* And me having to pony up a halvsie, not just a *thirdsy?*

'You guys are fucking crazy and I want nothing to do with you!'

Exactly what I should have said. But the CEO in me saw opportunity. If I enabled them, if I took them to the brink of it actually happening, I could get Bo Leemic busted for conspiracy to murder. Nothing shabby about that. And Bullies Inc. needed a triumphant return after my demoralizing strike out with Al Kida. It would also end my corporation's bully ridding competition. 'I can get some, but not the whole thous… grand.'

Another round of high-fives and this time Courtney raised a hand. I hate the fucking gesture, but when in Rome… Once through with the bullshit ceremony they asked if I had any money on me so they could buy some weed. A pair of lowbrow mooches. As we started making our way from the woods I let my eager weed-craving partners forge ahead and then edged to a stop. I turned back and took a look around. In that leafy blackness, someone was there.

48

I was able to track down the license plate
from the car at the strip club. It was registered to a
lawyer who had a wife and three kids, a boy and two
daughters. I assumed it was the older daughter in the
car with him and the stripper, the same girl I'd seen
pass out in the restaurant, the one Guy-Dick claimed
was the ringleader of a group called Bullies Inc. I
checked to see if the name was registered. Bullies Inc.
was not registered, but due diligence is just that.

I needed to learn more about this girl, perhaps
surveil her as I had Courtney, but that kind of thing
took a lot of time. As well, I had no clue to who the girl
named in the second letter, Bo Leemic, really was, or if
she'd already been 'realigned.' Opportunity was
dropping through my fingers.

I decided to jump straight in and confront the girl,
the ringleader, the Svengali, Dolph, and present her
with everything Guy-Dick had told me, then squeeze
from her a confession. I learned the lawyer's oldest
daughter was working in the same restaurant the
waitress worked, the friend of Courtney I'd met at her
mother's house. It took the better part of a day before I
realized the one working there was in fact the lawyers'
older daughter, but she wasn't the one I saw faint, or
the one in the car that night at the strip club. I'd blown
another entire day.

I followed the older sister to her home, and decided
to set up surveillance the next morning on Dolph.

49

No turn un-stoned

Fuck those chicks could smoke dope! That night I fake-inhaled, but under Bo and Courtney's suspicious glares down went several combustive hits of THC. The smoke clouded me; the drug overtook and overwhelmed me. In the girl's twisted grins I saw blood lust – in their half-moon eyes I saw murderousness – they were about to –

After they demolished the last of my bankrolled dope their talk of slaughtering Anna Rexic, and a good many others slithered into fantasies of riches and hot men and easy living. Listening to their mindless illusions cost me more brain cells than the drugs ever could.

We hooked up the next morning and straight away they started in on me getting the 1000$ for Anna's 'Whacking.' Rather than chance them raising their *halvsie* of five hundred$ and offering it to the gang dude along with their bodies, thusly cutting me out (probably seen too many crimes shows) I told them I'd fund the entire thousand. I stalled them with more drug $ and once they were good and stoned informed them before I turned over any more $, I'd first have to meet the dude. The killer.

Their immediate retort, 'No.'

My immediate retort, 'No deal.'

As I walked away my new BFFs were suddenly flanking me, pleading for me to stay and talk things out. I knew this wasn't so much about the money, it was the fact I shared their murderous secret and could do with it as I pleased. Their stoner half-moon eyes were ablaze, much like adult blow-up dolls as they continued on for my understanding. And in their feebleness I realized I too was stoned. On power.

A breathless deal was brokered, they promising to set up a meeting with the would-be-assassin and me promising not to tell anyone about it, and to keep working on the $.

50

-6:02 AM. Arriving I park my car half a block from my subject Dolph's house. The sun has yet to break the horizon or begin to burn off the morning haze. Surveillance is underway. There are no lights on in the house or in most of the surrounding houses.

-6:07 AM. I find myself in an excruciation of immobility and boredom. I've never been one to sit still. Even sick with the flu I often pace my apartment until my body gives out and I'm forced back to bed.

-6:22 AM. No activity in or around the house. Surf the net for the latest articles on bullying. All are painfully standard, parents blaming the school, the school blaming the parents or lack of witnesses and always their scrawny budgets. All the more reason to see this through.

-6:45 AM. A second-floor light pops on. I throw all attention on Dolph's house.

-7:11 AM. A first-floor light comes on. A shadow lurks behind drawn sheers. Another first-floor lights pops on, then another. Then nothing.

-7:58 AM. The lawyer father exits my subject's home, gets into an MG Spitfire sports car and presumably leaves for work.

-8:27 AM. I continue surveillance, one eye on the house the other on my device. Forever being a last minute Xmas shopper I've promised myself to get it done before the onslaught of advertiser indulgence which begins the morning after Hallowee – The mother and older sister and younger brother bustle out the front door get into a blue Subaru station wagon and drive away down the street. I'm now alone with my subject.

-9:19 AM. I worry Dolph isn't there. Possibly slept over at a friend's? No I remember Guy-Dick telling me she's a total loner. I flash memories of myself as a teen.

-10:02 AM. Around me the street's alive with joggers, gardeners and a group of kids playing ball-hockey.

-10:14 AM. The sun has made a magnifying glass of my windshield and turned my car into an oven. Stupidly I left my windows rolled up for cover. I cannot risk turning on the air conditioner as my running motor could give me away.

-10:48 AM. This heat – sweat funnels down my chest and spine my vision blurs I have little choice but to risk cracking a window. I key the car battery alive and ease my finger against the button Nnnzip! it blasts further down than I want, exposing me. I reverse it but it shuts tight, the dammed buttons have no slow speed and I never realized how loud they are NNNNNZZZZIP! NNNNNZZZZZIP!!

-11:01 AM. BANG! A hockey ball hammers off my driver's door and my head hammers off the roof. I see stars.

-11:39 AM. Nature has run its course I'm just brain and bladder one working to control the other.

-11:52 AM. Discomfort has become pain. Lisa Nowak enters my mind, the astronaut who on a cross-country dash to her lover wore adult diapers to stave off any washroom stops.

-12:13 PM. My surging bladder is waterboarding my vital organs. I key the ignition and gear my car for the closet washroom – heading out from the house, Dolph. I watch her make her way down the street and pass me and pray she's heading somewhere there's a washroom or leafy woods. I ease over speed bumps as if about to explode. Dolph stops and turns back and looks straight at me. I pass her and carry on down the block. At the corner I look back. She's gone.

I drive around taking corner after corner but find no sign of her. I pull over and lean onto my steering wheel. I've blown it.

-12:38 PM. I race into a gas station/convenience mart. Relief has never felt so good. But then disillusionment. I order a large coffee and go back to my car and tally any possibility of compiling a story. My so-called breakout story. I open my window and begin to pour out the vile coffee and heading out from the convenience store with a coffee and breakfast sandwich – Dolph!

She stops and turns and again meets my stare. Window down I'm entirely exposed and not only is Dolph staring at me, but beside her, also eyeing me, are Courtney and the waitress. I shift into first and ease my vehicle into – a line up for a carwash. If I back out of the line I'll attract attention so I wait my turn, neck crooked, trying to keep them in sight. My car is hooked and dragged and Dolph and the girls disappear behind a jet of white soapy foam.

-12:51 PM. My car's finally released from the manacle and as the last of the rinse runs down the windows my eyes jag from one corner of the lot to the other. Dolph and girls are nowhere. I don't deserve this story.

-1:01 PM. I reread the letter Dolph has written me, warning of the girl Bo Leemic's demise. Tears begin to flow.

-1:11 PM. Just as I put my car in gear for home and defeat, the waitress, Courtney, and Dolph exit the convenience store.

51

Good girls go to heaven. Bad girls go wherever they want.

Upon leaving my house I walked past a car and thought I recognized the woman slumped down behind the wheel trying her dearest to look inconspicuous. If I wasn't entirely certain she was the reporter, by the time I turned back and studied the 'caught' look on her face, I was. With the poor creature clearly in need of help I made my path an open one, as in easy to follow, just shy of leaving a trail of breadcrumbs. At one point I even doubled back in an effort to help her truly terrible surveillance but she appeared to have lost me. Or perhaps her showing up at the gas station long after I'd met up with the girls was no fluke and she wasn't all that terrible?

I cringed. Not from making barefaced eye contact with Ms. Reporter, but in her effort to escape our connection she drove straight into the carwash lineup. Bo Leemic asked, then demanded to know what the fuck I was laughing about (as well as their previously mentioned qualities bullies are narcissistic, believing everything is about them). Rather than tell her a novice reporter was following us, a story from the night before proved the perfect distraction.

My Aunt Sylvia was over for dinner and martinis, she being the only martini imbiber, and at the table she tipsily announced her son was starting community college. She announced it as if her precious boy had single-handedly purified the oceans. Perhaps she'd forgotten telling us of his three previous ventures into the world of community college, and his subsequent trio of expulsions. Spawned from her fourth marriage this was the same son who lost his summer job in an old-folks home. Not because he got drunk on the midnight shift and was found the next morning passed out in one of the trauma baths, no, it was because he drunkenly believed sneaking into twenty-three rooms and playing musical chairs with the old folk's teeth, moving them from bedside-glass to bedside-glass without keeping track of whose was whose, would spawn nothing but hilarity!

At the dinner table renegade beads of pity were leaking from my family's strained looks. Aunt Sylvia turned her booze-reddened nose and eyes on me, probably because I displayed the least interest, and rhetorically asked if I'd be coming to her cherished son's graduation? 'No thanks Aunt Sylvia. But count me in for his next parole hearing.' Banished to my room I stayed there until the morning when all pandemonium broke loose.

That summer my brother spun an idea in his head. Any poison in the world was due him. Salmonella in Oregon—destined for his bloodstream. Tainted chicken in India – already coursing through his nervous system. Contaminated carrots in East Prussia—buy him a headstone. After brushing his teeth that morning Mr.

Hypochondriac read the toothpaste tube, you know the engraving at the base (who does that?) and saw it had passed its expiry date by two and a half weeks!

Baby bro went into an apoplectic meltdown and could only be pacified by my mother and sister rushing him to the hospital. I wasn't directly involved in any of the pandemonium, still in my bedroom from the night before I listened to it through the vent and was glad to be forgotten because had I not, I feared being asked to go to the hospital to which I'd have answered, 'No thanks. But count me in for little bro's funeral.'

Back at the gas station Bo and Courtney were between a sweat-and-shit clamoring to go and find our hired hitman. They had no way of raising him on the phone because Mr. Hired Killer used burner phones he changed on a weekly basis. So while the girls were trying to drag me off, I'm watching Ms. Reporter's car get swallowed into the carwash and doing my best to stall the girls, to the point of going back into the store and lavishing them with even more leaden breakfast snacks. If you're wondering why I wanted Ms. Reporter around, that morning as I saw her skulking behind the wheel of her car it hit me, the utter perfection in her being there. I could lead her straight to Bo and Courtney and their murderous plan, and have an adult be witness to it.

Leaving the gas station Bo Leemic, Courtney, myself, and an undeclared guest headed out into our destinies.

52

Luck was with me. Not only was I able to retrace Dolph who was still with Courtney and the waitress, but their next move was boarding a bus. Following a bus was much easier than following someone on foot.

Dolph led her companions to the back seat. Eyes generally on the girls, she'd occasionally glanced back to the street. The drive became tedious, me stopping behind the bus, waiting for it to re-launch, then driving as quickly or more often, as slowly as it did. I became oblivious to where I was. But that ended when the girls exited the bus at the mouth of the city projects.

Dolph followed Courtney and the waitress into the maze of scarred buildings. I struggled to find a parking spot, and hoped my car would be there when I got back and not up on blocks or gone. That might sound stereotypical, but reputations are garnered for a reason, and one of the two cars I parked between was on blocks, its charred interior long burned out. A group of men huddled about, their gazes alerted to the girls who were breaking a path towards one of the high-rises. The land looked as if it had been bulldozed for farmland. Level enough for police cruisers was my guess. Why use your legs when you could drive? I have a love/hate relationship with the police.

The girls gathered outside the lobby of one the eleven towers, each indecipherable from the other.

City planning's finest hour. I also have a love/hate relationship with city politics and the ghettoization of the underclass. Using a pair of binoculars, I found I didn't have to leave the car which was a relief. The waitress went inside and came right back out. The three girls stood anxiously outside the lobby. A couple of men approached them and began to strike up a conversation. One of the men peered about, leaving me with a feeling of dread. Dolph eased back, and looked to be setting herself apart from the gathering.

BANG!

BANG!

Again I was startled into the ceiling of my car! Crouched down and gripping my head I peeked over the dashboard. Another bang, sounding like a gunshot, then another. The group of men was hunched down, hands disappearing into their clothing. A car cruised past. Two teens hung out the back windows lighting off cannon crackers and tossing them in the air. Some of the group rose from their hunches and raced towards them. The car burned rubber on its exit, both parties throwing hand signs and curses to each other.

Looking back towards the building I watched a man, I guessed a teen, exit abeen talking to the girls and they drifted back to their former gathering. The teen boy walked off with the girls, Dolph lagging behind.

I started my engine and looking up found a gang of men surrounding my car. One started pounding on my window.

53

The Devil You Blow

They rose from the earth like a bad dream, eleven twenty-story towers I'd seen only from afar, or on the news. Getting off the bus I followed Bo and Courtney across the street that seemed to separate one side of town from the other. I marveled at the girls' lack of trepidation; where their footsteps seemed impatient for the concrete jungle, mine posed ready to turn and run.

Once within them we were cut off from the sun. Trailing behind the girls I watched their seeming impatient steps turn into something of a swagger. A group of men looked us over then two broke from the others and headed our way. Their walk would have been more threatening if they weren't doing limo-strides in order to keep their pants up. It wasn't the time for jokes but my mind has always had a mind of its own. I hate falling to cliché but I broke a sweat waiting for these dudes to reach into the back of their jeans, you know for their 'piece' their 'gat' but they never did. They were, in a word, Cool. Didn't try and sell us crack or meth or flamethrowers or missile launchers or anything TV liked to portray of the projects, they just wanted to know what we were doing there; protecting their turf was how I read it. Now I don't mean these grim-faced gentlemen rolled out the red carpet, but once Bo told them who we were there to see they left us unscathed. In hindsight, I realized the truly dangerous people are the overtly friendly. A smile can hide more than any frown.

I looked around for Ms. Reporter, but she was nowhere to be seen. Part of me couldn't blame her, but for fuck sakes, bitch, sometimes you just gotta get down in the trenches! Bo had already buzzed our project killer and we waited for him under the attention of our two grim-faced friends and the gaze of about a dozen other men and counting. Non-stop talkers Bo and Courtney prattled on and on and on. Why is it the ones who speak the most say the least? I fantasized sealing their mouths shut.

Silence is golden. Duct-tape is silver.

Project killer finally showed up, strutting through the lobby as if his 5ft 5, maybe 5ft 4 scrawny testosterone-fueled frame held the deed to the building. What shall I call him? Les Semen. Now Les Semen, maybe all 14 or 15 years of him, had a multitude of life philosophies, his 'Nez' as he called it (dat's Zen *'clevaly'* spelt 'ackwards) and as far as he was concerned each was a pearl of brilliance in a protracted necklace of genius. 'Live the life you lead, and leave no dude standin' in your way.' It appeared not only danger lived in the projects but something far, far worse. Teen pretention. I counted myself lucky he at least wasn't 'rhymin' his philosophies.

He led us to the other side of that street (the sunny side?) and into a greasy spoon he considered his 'second crib,' where he high-fived it with a bunch of his pants-limboing homies. Having wrestled ourselves into a sticky booth we listened as he further expounded 'Nez' in one uninterrupted exasperatingly longwinded diatribe. I lost track of time to the point of trying to gauge the earth's revolution. I felt my brain gnawing on itself like an animal caught in a trap. Precious time and brain cells forever lost. And if I thought the situation couldn't get any worse I was sorely mistaken, because just about the time my brain was going to chew through its last bits of cartilage and stagger bloodily from the trap, Les Semen began rhymin'!

FUCK! So there I was being rhythmically impaled by musings of less caliber than common shithouse etchings. Unable to stand anymore I decided to test Mr. Semen. Breaking into his harangue I asked, 'Does it count as a pistol-whipping if the gun's still in its factory sealed box?' The question stunned both him and the girls.

Avoiding any kind of answer, Les Semen continued his verbal ejaculations (just had to say that) while my anguished brain conjured multiple layers of silver duct tape fixed round his mouth – Just then my phone rang. Before I could begin to read the display, I claimed it was my parents calling from the hospital and rushed outside. Turned out the one who saved me from the rhymin', stomach-turnin' philosophizin', my shiny White Knight was none other than Guy-Dick!

I figured Mr. Dick to be long out of the country, living under a pseudonym in Mexico or Paraguay, but he was making a local call. Seemed Guy-Dick was in the midst of raising money for something I came to know as his 'Mohawk circumcision!' I'll pay the idea no more space.

He'd also been making pen pals of women inmates from the local prison and was now dogging a fresh discharge. He said after being locked up for a year she was so ravenous for a taste of manhood it was like sticking it in a Cuisinart. His charm had not abated, but I had to give him credit for using the word 'Manhood' and not one of his other aliases for it, 'The Egg Beater,' 'The Paralyzer,' 'GERONIMO,' etc. etc. In any case he was calling to ask if I was still in the business of bully realigning because this fresh discharge was 'Chomping on the bit' (Guy failed to see any irony in that) to do a job on a bully. I looked back into the restaurant. Bo Leemic and Courtney continued to be enraptured by Les Semen's versin' and coercin'.

I confirmed an immediate meeting with Guy who seemed to be making an effort to transition himself from porn star to jailbird pimp, and I'll call her... 7574365 (not her real inmate number) then hung up and texted Bo that myself and my $ were outta there as I'd found a more viable option. I had to clarify – perhaps I should have rhymed my text – what I meant by 'viable option' then further clarify I'd have nothing more to do with Les Semen. So enraptured with himself Mr. Semen didn't notice Bo and Courtney sharing my texts and not until they were halfway to the door did he stop and look up from his phone; as well as rhymin' his conceited platitudes, Les Semen had been texting the entire time.

Just then I noticed Ms. Reporter across the street in the parking lot, her car surrounded by a gang of men. In her fluster, I was reminded of a dream I'd had the night before. My mother sent me to the store for milk, and when I opened the cooler all the cartons, not just the milk ones but the 18% 10% and 5% cream cartons, the chocolate milk cartons, even the juice cartons had my frowning picture on them with a reward posted not for my return, but my imprisonment.

54

Six of them rocked my car, demanding to know who I was and what the @%#*& I was doing in their hood. Heart in my mouth I reached for the city map I had on the passenger seat hoping to show them I was lost then—BANG! A gunshot. And for a third time that morning my head bashed into the roof. Again I saw stars. When my vision finally cleared the men were gone, chasing a car, the same one as before, back for a second launching of cannon crackers. I threw my vehicle into reverse and peeled away.

I drove out in search of the girls. Eventually I found Dolph standing outside a strip-mall on her phone. Then, exiting a restaurant, the waitress and Courtney joined her.

What had happened with the teen boy? Had some kind of deal brokered? Had they purchased a firearm? I followed the girls back across town, and where did they lead me? Straight to Guy-Dick. This time Guy was not alone, with him was a woman, small in stature, and not un-pretty in a steely kind of way. The five of them, Dolph, Courtney, the waitress, Guy, again I'll defer to my co-author's synonym, 7574365, headed into some woods. I had no choice but to follow on foot. Though I'd just escaped a gang scare in the projects, whatever I was heading into then felt even worse.

55

Gall that Glitters

Guy's new GF, 7574365 was not at all what I'd imagined. I pictured horribly tattooed prison-gristle, her hard-bitten face sporting Jack-o-lantern teeth. But this creature was almost dainty in appearance and, save for the gold-capped incisor that occasionally caught the sun and reflected back a gilded beam, she could have passed for one of my neighbors. But then again, I have neighbors like stripper-Mandy. Prison creature seemed pleasant enough until Guy (wearing a T-shirt that boasted, *Here's to all virgins: THANKS FOR NOTHING!*) raised the subject of bullies. At this she transformed into a cyclone of rage and launched into her personal history, one of great tragedy... bet'ya didn't see that coming:

No clue of her father. Mother was a boozer. Touched by her Uncle. Touched by her Uncles. Met and fell in love with a non-family trailer-parker named Lonnie who pimped her out to a local strip club, and when she refused to do more than hand-jobs good-old Lonnie slashed the tires of her trailer and set it on fire...

'An' I paid fur 'em! I paid fur's teeth!' LONNY YA FUCKIN' BASTERD! I PAID FUR YER GODDAMN TEETH!!!'

There was just no Hallmark card for the moment.

Her screaming having chased away a migration of winged life and a handful of sunbathers, 7574365 turned back to us. We waited, as one might for an aftershock and our patience was soon rewarded. Bellowing, 'Then ya went an' fucked the den'ist's dog-faced nurse (I believe she meant dental-technician, but I didn't feel the moment appropriate to quibble over semantics) 'and ya gam'me the 'Herp!'

The *Herp?* How could anyone not love this woman!

Guy-Dick's arm was suddenly around her in a way I thought somewhat unwholesome. Pimpish. But the situation was proving perfect; a con just out of prison with a chip on her shoulder hired to off a bully – well isn't that just the North American way?

All I had to do was make sure Ms. Reporter was following the crime and voilà, Bullies Inc. would once again reign triumphant! I turned to Bo and Courtney who seemed transfixed by 7574365's ranting gold-toothed glimmer and whispered they best start negotiations with her because I refused to cough up a penny for Les Semen.

Seeing the three girls approach each other reminded me of sniffing dogs. Would they take a whiff and ignore each other? Play with each other? Fight to the death? They were soon in a heated discussion I purposely kept apart from. You see, if I kept free from the details and didn't know exactly what was going on, I couldn't be tried for anything. As I said before, being CEO I needed to look forward, be ahead of the curve. In the spirit of this I decided when I did cough up the $, rather than hand it over to both girls I'd pass it only to Bo, and even then, not directly. As they came to a deal I followed Guy's gaze to 7574365's post prison spandex pants that gave her the appearance of having just sat on an axe.

56

Hiding amongst some shrubbery I felt less a journalist and more a peeping Tom. Using binoculars to appear a bird watcher, I forced smiles to the few who walked by, and the same to a sudden scattering of sunbathers. The new girl with the gold tooth entirely took over the proceedings, ranting and raving, and Dolph, to my surprise, let it happen. Then 7574365, the waitress and Courtney huddled together. They were too quiet to hear but a plan seemed to be being hatched. Soon after Dolph and the girls left, leaving me alone with 7574365 and Guy.

Who to follow? Dolph was my primary, but my gut said stick to 7574365 because whatever had gone down was serious and she was calling the shots. I was torn, but then fate interceded. Right there in the clearing Guy-Dick and 7574365 started making out, and her abrupt drop to her knees sent me back after Dolph, with Guy-Dick's words echoing through the brush: 'Ahhhh, careful baby, it's not made'a jerky!'

I searched around, but I'd lost the girls. Arriving at my car I found pinned under the windshield wiper blade another red envelope. The letter inside stated there would be another 'realigning,' only this one would be 'permanent.' I looked about but the lot was empty.

Clearly, I was being played. If I went to the police I would either look like a naïve, desperate reporter, or if they believed me and took action too soon, all involved would claim it a hoax and my story would fall to pieces. But if I kept quiet and it did go down, I'd be accomplice to a murder.

57

GETTING MY FUCKS IN A ROW

Prisoner of our family dinner, I listened to big sis prattle on about how, through her conscientious-objecting to any retaliation against Bo Leemic, she had won. This shrewd observation garnered from the fact her enemy was now ignoring her which could mean only one thing, Ms. Leemic had seen the light and the errors of her ways. Choking on sis's illusory bullshit, I looked across the table and asked younger brother if there was any more of the past-its-date toothpaste? He revived his morning hysterics and, with the table in an uproar, I quietly slid out for the evening.

The night air was growing cooler; summer was coming to an end. I was neither glad nor sad of this; seasons are simply unavoidable so why get upset about them? I went to a phone booth to call Bo Leemic. Do they ever clean those fucking things? It was a wasteland of soiled wrappers, crushed cigarette butts and the receiver so caked with people's stale breath and gunge I wasn't sure my voice would even penetrate it. After some small talk Bo asked why I was talking so loud? I lowered my voice and took over suggesting Courtney wasn't up to how crucial the next part of our endeavor was and convinced Ms. Leemic she should become the primary participant, her being the stronger and smarter of the two. While she basked in my fabrication I further convinced her we should have no more face to face contact and for her to pick up the money alone. She gushingly agreed.

Television, could there be a better source for mastering criminal behavior? When I was younger my dad used to snuggle me up on the couch and we'd watch crime movies on the late show (though he cringed at the thought of criminals in real life, dad seemed okay with law-breakers on celluloid). I loved those old black and whites where, whenever anyone was punched or slapped, man or woman, they'd end up with that same dribble of blood running down one corner of their mouth. I mean even if they were kicked in the shin or stubbed their toe, there's that same dribble of blood running down one corner of their mouth. And whenever the bad guy said anything important he followed it with a sharp, 'Nyea, see!' Just like hipsters do now, only theirs follow blabbing of no importance, every sentence butted with the infuriatingly leaden, 'Ya know?' A 'Ya know?' they never wait for an answer to.

Drawing on one of those old film clichés I had Bo retrieve the money from a bus station locker. I haven't mentioned this but Ms. Leemic was extremely germ-a-phobic, refusing handshakes, hugs, forever slathering her hands with sanitizer, even refusing the free meals offered by the restaurant she worked, fearing the dishwashing unit wasn't up to code. What better place to break her from her neurosis than a crowded and transitory bus station. I put the envelope of 500$, which I'd recorded the bill's serial #s, into the dirtiest locker I could find, left the key taped to the back of the women's washroom toilet tank then bounced up to the second-floor atrium. The open balcony made it easy for me to spy Bo, and left plenty of room for Ms. Reporter, on the first floor disguised under baseball cap – a real chameleon – to spy me.

Watching Bo was better than any of those old crime movies, clearly she'd never graced the terminal with her presence. Narrowing herself or inching sideways she weaved to avoid its transients as if brushing against one might cause her some horrible malignancy. She exited the washroom as though being chased, and opening the locker snatched the envelope of money, slammed the door shut and ran out, hands freaking into her purse for sanitizer. The only thing missing was the dribble of blood running down one corner of her mouth.

I'd made everything within walking distance. So while I followed Bo, Ms. Reporter followed me for about five blocks to a diner where not only 7574365 was waiting, but Anna Rexic had taken a job; putting on the act of being a worthwhile citizen for the courts. This one-stop shopping meant Bo could drop the retainer and I.D. Ms. Rexic to 7574365. Following my instructions Bo made it clear to 7574365 that if Guy-Dick was any way involved in this, I would call the whole thing off. I figured him too squeamish to let it get far enough along. And with all participants being women... well doesn't the mind just wander...

58

Sowing what you reap

The time had come for me to step back. I needed to distance myself from the next night, and staying home would create an alibi. I just had to hope Bo and 7574365 would follow through, and Ms. Reporter took the situation seriously enough to show up and call the cops before it went too far. I did not want this to lead to Anna Rexic's murder, but I absolutely needed it to lead to Bo Leemic's demise. The location and time had been set; all I had to do was get some sleep and wait the next day out.

I fell into a shitty sleep and woke absolutely wired. By 10 that morning I'd paced a trail into the carpets and dulled a path along the hardwood with my perspiry feet. The ringing had me leaping out of my skin. If there was ever a time I wanted to kill a telemarketer, reach through the phone and dig my fingers into their eerily-pleasant-telephone-voice throats...

Back to pacing I tripped over a carpet-runner and found myself face down on the floor. As I lay in a fury of self-pity, I could feel every tick of the clock amputating another second of life I would never get back.

In time I hauled my pitiful ass from the floor and down to the rec room, to the one grace that might help my endless day – Jerry Springer. You can always count on Jerry and his dimwitted guests for an hour of distracting entertainment that inevitably leaves you feeling better about yourself. Go Jerry! Time flew, me sharing the agony and the ecstasy of the toothless and the profane, the hair-pulling, wig-discarding battlements dovetailing into the soothing resonance of Jerry's final thought. A 2:00PM newsflash scrawled across the screen. 2:00PM? THAT'S 8 MORE FUCKING HOURS!

Clearly the sands of time where mocking me. The same way my Uncle mocks his in-laws, 'You look happier Gladys, I can see by all those new creases in your face.' The reprieve I'd gained from Jerry Springer quickly vanished. Anxiety was back haunting me, shadowing me throughout the house from room to room like some torturous ghost. Outside the day was beautiful, the kind of day one should be out in and enjoying. The kind they go on about in pretentious novels: *The warm solstice breeze fanned the grand oak tree like so many angel wings, and as the sunlight dabbled its emerald leaves and danced through the meadow of sumptuous grass, the sight blessed a kind of spell on me, one where all in the world was good.* Stepping out into that *sumptuous* day felt like stepping into a trap. My stay in the all-good world was fleeting.

I scanned the channels for more Jerry (I wondered if 7574365 had ever appeared, she seemed born for it). Again and again I found it, again and again my fingers flew to the remote, and again and again the same fucking episode. They've been doing the show for over 20 fucking years you'd think they could play a different one for fuck sakes! The thought of watching the same one again made me feel even more pathetic.

I grabbed my phone and scrolled down to Bo's #. I needed to talk to her. I needed to know how things were progressing. Again and again my thumb hovered over the send button, longed into it, but CEO sensibility stopped me – the contact could later be traced. I bolted to the kitchen and found myself tearing though the fridge despite the fact I wasn't remotely hungry or thirsty. I understood how some people get fat; bored or anxious people needing to load up on sugary sodas or precooked food in order to choke back the appalling boredoms and anxieties that erupt within us. I walked away from that Freon Temptress, maintaining my figure but feeling worse.

With no idea of how I got there, I found myself standing in front of my parents' medicine cabinet. I scanned its boxes and bottles – both glass and plastic – read the warnings, measured the little I knew of medicines and drugs against what I felt or was trying not to feel, and I took the most potent drug in the cabinet. Waiting for it to take effect I re-paced the house the way you might re-trace your footsteps in deep snow in order to avoid the chore of breaking new ground. That, and I wanted to reclaim each previous step with ones of confidence.

I didn't.

Outside, the brilliant day continued blossoming while inside the day continued darkening. I found myself running down to the rec room and to the couch where my phone lay. I pressed send. And in the milliseconds I waited for contact I felt I aged ten years. I hung up cursing my wretched weakness. And as I sat on the floor (I no longer felt worthy of the couch) I found my medicine cabinet cure kicking in. My stomach was settling down from a fast burn to a slow simmer; the antacids performing as promised. And yes, extra-strength antacids were the most potent drugs in the medicine cabinet, my parents being absolute proponents of a pill-less living.

Again I demeaned myself to the diversion of television. Knees clenched to my chin I flicked around rolling up and down the legion of satellite channels (really only about 30 channels with teams of affiliates repeating the same fucking shows) but found nothing diverting. I ended up flipping between a medical documentary that sent microscopic cameras into all orifices of the human body—Nice. And a celebrity 'Reality' show where some past-their-prime luminaries invite camera crews into their house in last-ditch efforts to remain in the public eye – Pathetic. I found myself contemplating how they might converge. I mean isn't it just a matter of time before one of those pathetic ego-feeding celebs in an effort to outdo one of their rival pathetic ego-feeding celebs in the age-old battle for television ratings lower themselves to showing private footage of say... Their recent colonoscopy? Looking even further ahead, is it not inevitable those wars would spawn some kind of scandal?

Breaking news – The colonoscopy footage our network aired last week was not really that of _____ (pathetic-celeb name). The mucky innards were actually those of his personal assistant. Our sincerest apologies.

I felt myself slipping into a fathomless chasm (kinda like that colonoscopy camera but without the light). Back in the kitchen I checked the clock (as if the one on my phone might be out to trick me) 4:06? 4-0-fucking-6! Though not having tripped over anything I again found myself on the floor.

My mind felt like it was glowing, like some sinister, nuclear waste had been drilled into my head. If I could've stuck a finger into my skull to make it vomit out my brain I'd not have hesitated. Staring into my cellphone, I contemplated its role in my grey-matter fallout. Had its sound waves of radiation fried it? Then the realization – I hardly used it. Then the realization – I didn't have many friends to call. Then the realization – I didn't have *any* friends to call. I had to reach out to someone –

'Guy? Hey, hi! Beautiful day outside isn't it? Yeah, it would be great for tanning. Two whole shades? How do you measure something like that – What? Yeah, I guess she was pretty hot. No I didn't know it was for robbery – A burger place, really? She stopped to order a burger first? Noooo, that's not so crazy...I guess. Well I mean if you're already robbing the place and you're hungry – No I wouldn't do it myself – Well either one, rob the place or stop for a burg – Maybe you should get out of the sun? Okay fine, one more shade.

Guy, so like you've known me for a bit, right? And... well...I – So what do you think of me? Do you think I'm likeable?

Guy?

Guy?

Guy?'

Even in an imaginary call where I could have made myself into anything I wanted, I was hung up on.

I must have exhausted myself. I woke at the foot of the rec room couch with night upon me. I bolted up the stairs in time to find our driveway doused in an array of flashing police lights.

59

A man shouldn't have to bust balls to get himself heard. But guess what? That's just what I had to do!

Guy-Dick is so not my real name. It's the name 'Dolph' made up for me. So I made up a name for her. Lil'-bitch. The first part's for little, and the bitch part seems pretty straightforward. I'm not asking if she likes it cause she didn't ask me if I liked mine. But chicks don't really want guy's opinions, not unless they're getting something from it, but that's the way the world turns. So I hooked up 7574365 and Lil'-bitch, and she brought along two fine little tighties, Courtney and Bo. I could clearly see them doing an act on each other, tongue-in-grooving, scissoring and whatnot.

When we hooked up Lil'-bitch said she was gonna pay 7574365 to do a number on some bully, just like I'd done. So anyway, with the cash I'd jet down to Mexico where I knew a guy who'd get me work in bar shows in Tijuana. Outstanding! So later on, 7574365 and I are getting it on and she's moaning and talking and out comes, 'I'm gonna end that bitch. GONNA KILL 'ER!'

Wha — Whoa, whoa the fuck up woman! So I

pull out, which really pisses her off, and ask her, 'What'd you just say?' So she gets all clammy and shit and pulls down her dress so I can see her face and says, 'Nothin'. I'm not supposed ta tell ya.'

So we leave the restaurant and she never shuts up. You know when a skirt talks and talks and talks so you can't get a word in because they don't want you to get a word in. So while she's blabbing on, and even though I hate cops, I started thinking about calling the cops. But the more I thought about it the more I realized they'd hog all the credit. And if anyone was going to save a life, jump in and be the hero of the piece, it was Guy-Dick! But how would I stop it? If I phoned Dolph and told her the 411 she'd probably shut it down. And where would I be then? I'll tell you, right back where I started, a thousand miles from the sweet sun of Tijuana. So fuck Dolph... Lil-bitch! I got that reporter on the phone, the uptight thing that didn't drink or screw. What the hell you saving it for honey???

I knew she wanted the story, wanted it real bad, probably the only thing in life she wanted real bad. So I tell her I'd give her the story, but only with me being the hero. Local Hero Risks Life in Saving Life! There's a headline! Guy-Dick busting

out his hero moves. Epic! Hero 1. Bitches 0. Oh
yea! So I say we need to meet, but Ms. Saving-it
says she can't. So I tell her if she doesn't,
someone she knows in her story is gonna die. But
even that's not good enough for Ms. All-important.
You ever take a look at that word, important? If
you take out one letter – R – you get impotent.
Except its tent on the end of impotent, not tant
like in important, but it's really close. So I tell
Ms. Saving-it, Ms. Impotent, some of what's going
on, but like just enough to whet her appetite,
probably the only thing in her that ever got wet,
and she says let's meet at so-and-so's restaurant.

You know, I kinda liked all this spy shit; you
can't mention a real place and you have to use
fake names. Not like I haven't used a fake name
or two. And I'll tell you something for sure; my
fake names were a lot better than Guy-Dick.

So I show up early cause I wanna see if she
shows up early, like all-important know-it-all's like
to do. Then they say you're late, even if it's only
half an hour and huff and mope like they've been
stood up for days. As many as I slam, I'll never
figure women out. So in she waltzes, all proud and
shit, but that don't mean shit to me, cause I'm
the hero of the piece! So I sit back and get my
own proud on and ask her, 'Sup?' She answers the

same; only I can tell she's never said it before cause how she says it is totally lame, '…sup…?' Pfffttt. So she presses me for more 411. Yeah baby bring it! I say we got some time, let's you buy Guy-Dick a drink. And while you're at it, buy one for yourself.

Club fucking soda and lemon? That's not a drink!? So I imagine Saving-it's club fucking soda and lemon filled with straight vodka, and every time she takes a drink I smile like, 'I know what ya want, and I know what ya really are.' Lol. I use that for Lying-Obvious-Lesbian.

So like there's only so much you can talk about if you're not trying to tap a chick. So I ask how she likes my tan, but I can tell she doesn't care one shit about my tan cause she's just thinking about no one but herself. Lol. Then she takes a drink, sucks it up through her straw. So I look over to the waitress and ask her for a straw and a steak. When she asks how I want the steak, I tell her like a hot colored chick – Black on the outside, pink on the inside! Then I slide the straw down into my drink and suck it like Saving-it did. Except I do it like I like doing it, cause my drink has taste. Club fucking soda and punk-ass lemon. Pfffttt!

So I'm down to the drippings of my chocolate

martini, sucking what's left from that little brown pucker of glass, but I'm cut short cause I have tell Ms. All-important to sit back down cause she's walking away from the best story of her life. On the street I'm chasing her and yelling after her to stop. Fucking women! I finally catch up to her and tell her I'll take her to where the thing was going down.

So there we were. Standing alone in the woods. Just the two of us. Two of us alone. So while we were waiting I'm thinking things. Her in a wedding-dress and when I lift it up to bang her, it covers her up so I don't have to look at her all-important face. Other shit too, but that'll be for my own book, the real story. Through the eyes of a Guy-Dick. The hero of the piece!

When the time was getting close, when it was supposed to go down, she made me tell her for like a third fucking time, everything I knew. So I tell her again and I'm like, 'You gotta spell my name right!' I made her punch it into her phone so I could make sure. No one fucks Guy-Dick over. Fucking club soda, punk-ass lemon bitch.

I thought of a whole lot of stuff while we waited there alone. Then I'd work it over and over in my head and change it so it got better and better. But she couldn't tell what I was doing. Lol!

That's the other lol. It was warm in the woods, like a hot summer night and I started getting a bloody. Some people call it a woody, but that's kid talk, got nothing to do with wood cause it fills with blood. So there I am all horny and shit, and then I look over to Saving-it and it shrank! Crawled up inside me the way it does whenever I watch Judge Judy or Nancy Grace.

It's real quiet. No traffic, no sounds of assholes on the street, just crickets and shit. Just us all alone. Not wanting to see her all-important-like face I look up at the sky, at the stars, not movie stars, the real stars.

'Orion.'

'What?'

She's looking right at me. So I point up to Orion and say, 'That.' She looks up to it, and when she looks back down her all-important look is gone. Like it weren't never there. She knew about them. Said her father taught her the stars, just like my friend's mom use to teach them to me. So we're pointing them out and trying to catch each other on who's wrong. Like, 'What's that one' and she'd say, 'Pictor.' And I'd say, 'Right!' Then she'd do it to me, and try and trip me up, but like not in a bad way. I don't think. She really knew her shit.

60

I sat on Dolph's house for most of the next day. Aside from her stepping out the side door, shielding violently from the sun and leaping back inside, nothing happened. I became worried she'd removed herself from any involvement, I'd miss the showdown and my chance to stop it. I got a call from Guy-Dick and, with no signs of Dolph about to leave the house, I felt little choice but to meet him.

It was to be a night of surprises. The first being my star-filled sky-bonding with Guy-Dick. Not in a million years could I have imagined myself shoulder to shoulder with him playing nametag with the constellations. But looking back on this story, it seems par for the course. The moon was nothing as dramatic as full, but as a big cloud dispersed, its light reflected into Guy's eyes. In one I could see a lens, not a contact lens, but one right inside his eye. I asked him about it. He became timid, shy, something I didn't think Guy-Dick capable of. He told me he had cataracts, that they ran in his family, and after clearing them from his one eye, they'd put in a lens for his vision. As I said, a night of surprises. Not only shy, he seemed downright sweet.

STEVE DIMARCO

Our moment was interrupted by bodies breaking through the undergrowth. From behind a thicket we watched two people enter a clearing. I recognized 7574365 right away, but with only photos to reference her, it took me a minute to identify Anna Rexic. She began looking around. 'Where is she? Where's Courtney?'

'I don't know,' 7574365 responded coldly. 'Where's Waldo?' I later learned 7574365 lured Anna to the park, claiming she could get Courtney to withdraw the charges of cyber-bullying. The police had discovered the child-porn on Anna Rexic's computer had been planted, but in the process found evidence of her online bullying, and with Courtney's consent, were charging Anna with cyber-bullying. Even from a distance I could see panic rising in Anna's face. 'Is she coming or what?'

Reaching under her jacket and into her spandex waistband 7574365 drew a large knife, a Bowie knife. Anna reeled back and went for her purse. And in a split second the waitress broke into the clearing waving a stun gun. 'Fuck you bitch!'

Just as Bo Leemic was taking aim on her, Anna Rexic produced her own stun gun (she later claimed getting death threats from being linked to child-porn, and had it for protection). Both girls fired on each other, both hit their marks. By then I'm dialing 911. The two girls fell to the ground, and as one was shocked, her finger would clench the trigger sending volts back into the other girl.

And this continued, over and over. I made my way into the clearing screaming the police were on their way. Guy was behind me, and when 7574365 saw him she screamed a streak of profanity, and threw her knife. I stepped aside in time to see its bone handle slam into Guy's crotch. Now three people were on the ground, one moaning, two convulsing.

By the time the police arrived the stun guns had discharged. Both girls, weapons still fixed in their grips, lay unconscious, and besides the occasional twitch, made for easy cuffing. Guy-Dick didn't understand why he was being cuffed, emphatically claiming, 'But I'm the hero of the piece!' My press-pass saved me from any metal restraints, but not a trip to the police station. Before I could say a word, Guy-Dick gave up Dolph to the cops, who picked her up and brought her in for questioning. If I couldn't make a breakout story from all this, I'd clearly chosen the wrong profession.

61

Alas

I'd not bear witness to all the enchanting conclusions. I'd only hear secondhand accounts of those final moments in the woods: the bitchy allegations, the nut-crunching knife throw, the twinned-stun-gunning climax to all my Bully Inc. labors. The hammer had come down on Bo Leemic and Anna Rexic and I could only imagine their expressions in being forced to look straight into the asshole of their bullying. Passing them in the police station hallway I was able to snag remnants of this, their sour, wretched looks, their sporadically twitching bodies. That must have really been something, their stun-gunning ping-pong tasing the other until their batteries went dead.

'NnnnZttt-'

'EEAAAHHHHHH!'

'NnnnZttt-'

'EEAAAHHHHHH!'

'NnnnZtttt-'

'EEAAAHHHHHH!'

Anna Rexic shrieked allegations that 7574365 (who disappeared after nut-sacking Guy-Dick) had gotten her involved. Courtney shrieked allegations Bo Leemic had gotten her involved. Bo Leemic shrieked allegations I'd gotten her involved and had been mastermind of the entire event. It was a nice compliment and quite true, though not well staged being we were all detainees in a police station where the air is always ripe with blame and finger pointing. Amid Bo's shrieked allegations I calmly shrugged ignorance. Ms. Leemic continued dispersing accusations not only against me, but against Courtney and 7574365. The old, rather tired looking detective, I'll call him Lance Boyle, couldn't make heads or tails of all that was being shrieked, only that two teen girls who'd been illegally carrying tasers (as well as some high-grade marijuana) had fired upon each other, a reporter had called it in, and the only male of the group was emphatically claiming, 'But I'm the hero of the piece!' The highlight was the morphing expressions of anger and fear and shame that coursed over everyone's faces.

The one expression I could have done without was my dad's. Watching him ushered into the interrogation room, he seemed to have aged. His face was sunken and blanched; his eyes darted about like confused moths trying to catch up with what Lance Boyle was telling him, or trying to tell him. I have to say the whole thing sounded even crazier from the mouth of that humorless old detective.

Bo Leemic and Anna Rexic were charged with possession of illegal tasers and released to their parents. Courtney was not charged and released to her mother. Unfazed by threats, they had ways to make him 'Stop-Talking,' Guy-Dick was ushered off to a holding cell. And me, valued readers, I was released to my father. Dear old Dad.

Sometime later, on my way home from school (by then I was a regular with the courthouse shrink dad had bestowed upon me) I found myself, once again, being followed, by Ms. Reporter. But this time, rather than scrunching down in her car seat and creeping behind me, she pulled up and got out and headed straight for me. No more sneaking around for Ms.! She fell in step with me and started walking me home. If she'd offered to carry my books it might have seemed a first date. Near my house she stopped and handed me a red envelope.

Inside was a piece of paper which I removed and unfolded. Ms. Reporter had drawn a kind of family tree. She'd lined up Bullies Inc.'s connection to everyone and everything, right back to Ralph and Joe and Van Detta, to Will and Goon 86, and of course Anna, Courtney, Bo and Guy-Dick. Each of these limbs were secured to the tree's trunk—me, Dolph. She'd traced every connection, every realigning, all of it provable in court. A vision of the interrogation room and dad's colorless face flooded back on me, my future passed before my eyes, each promising image slammed behind another iron door. Short of breath I leaned against a tree for support.

'Dolph, I don't think what you did was right,' she said. 'But...I don't think it was exactly wrong either.'

From my disintegration, I risked a look up.

'But in case you think about rebooting Bullies Inc., I've got all this information, and I've got these.' She produced my three letters.

Ms. was backlit by the sun giving her a preposterously perfect halo. Only when I squinted could I read her expression. It showed no signs of trickery. But how could I ever be certain?

62

My plan had the desired effect. Confronted with all she'd done the young vigilante looked on the verge of throwing up, fainting, or both. I'd never much considered vigilantism, certainly never been close to it. As well as its pitfalls, I could see its merits; quick effective retribution for someone wronged. It's a bit naïve to think the police can constitute all law and order. It's also naïve to think rampant vigilantism is a viable alternative. I went into it thinking black and white, and found only grey. I imagined pressing young Dolph for a written confession I could hold against her, but seeing her on the verge of collapse, I decided not to, her resigned nod was enough. I left her there.

So what about my breakout story? Unquestionably I had one. But what would it do? Sure, it would help my career, but at the same time it would kill a young girl's future. And would I report that too? Would I follow up that justice had been served because now this young, somewhat misguided entrepreneur would be labeled a violent offender for the rest of her life? Had she killed the helpless? Robbed the aged? Tortured babies? No, she did something about an injustice that despite all the attention, and all the political rhetoric heaved on it; shows no sign of abating.

Clearly I'd chosen the wrong profession. I stayed in it a while longer, but without that merciless drive reporting needs, the game lost its allure. I will not say what I'm doing now, but safe to say my change of careers has left my mother breathing a great sigh of relief.

63

Inanutshell

Gramps used to say, 'Never look a gift horse in the mouth!' I'd never really thought the expression through; but it's from an era when horses with bad teeth were not great gifts. I never did get a look into Ms. Reporter's mouth, and I have to live with that.

My Bullies Inc. road of progress had run into a cul-de-sac. So before its momentum curved back and ran over me, I hit the brakes and shut'r-down. I pondered flipping the corporation to some up-and-comer, you know, share my history and wisdoms and vicariously watch bullies fall to hands other than my own. But that was another mouth I would not to look into.

And in all my illegal activities, what had saved me, what had proven my one true ally? An Adult. Who'da thunk it? Ms. Reporter turned out to be the coolest most reasonable adult I'd ever met.

And that most definitely calls for a final 'excramation'!

acknowledgments:

James   Who pressed me to read novels

Rebecca   Who pressed through all my drafts

Mitze   Who helps me believe

Heidi   Who believes in this novel

and
Jocelyn
Who believes in me,
in all my goodnesses,
and in all my faults.